Taking a Gamble

By the Author

From This Moment On

True Confessions

Missing

Trusting Tomorrow

Desperate Measures

Up the Ante

Taking a Gamble

Taking a Gamble

by

PJ Trebelhorn

2016

TAKING A GAMBLE

ISBN 13: 978-1-62639-542-8

This Trade Paperback Original Is Published By
Bold Strokes Books, Inc.
P.O. Box 249
Valley Falls, NY 12185

First Edition: May 2016

Credits
Editor: Cindy Cresap
Production Design: Susan Ramundo
Cover Design By Sheri (graphicartist2020@hotmail.com)

Acknowledgments

First of all, a huge thank you to Radclyffe and to everyone who works behind the scenes at Bold Strokes Books. I can't imagine a better company to write for, and I'm truly honored to be a part of the Bold Strokes family.

To Sandy Lowe, thank you for everything you do. You rock!

To Sheri, another awesome cover. You never fail to impress.

To my amazing editor, Cindy Cresap, thank you for making me a better writer.

And last, but certainly not least, thank you, the reader. If not for you, there would be no reason to write.

Dedication

For Cheryl, for always being there

Chapter One

Cassidy Holmes sat at her small kitchen table, her oversized coffee mug nestled between her hands, and stared out the window. The dark snow clouds were keeping the rising sun at bay, and she sighed. Gordy, her two-year-old golden retriever, echoed her sentiments.

"I love the winter, but this year's been too much even for me, Gordy," she told him. She smiled when his ears perked up and he tilted his head in his best *I'm trying really hard to understand what you're saying* expression. She felt bad for him. He loved bounding through the snow and making tunnels, but he was getting tired of it too. They were on pace to break the record for the coldest February in over sixty years. And the snow. God, she was sick of having to use the snow blower what seemed like every day just to keep a clear path to her brother's house only seventy-five yards from her front porch.

After giving the dog a good scratch behind his ear, she took her mug to the sink before heading to the front door of her cabin. This was what she absolutely hated the most. Having to bundle up in snow pants, boots, gloves, hat, and jacket just to be able to take Gordy out to do his business.

The wind chill had been brutal most days of the month, and there was a part of her that was happy the storage auction business had all but halted for the winter. There were days she'd have gladly told her brother, Danny, to go fuck himself if there had been any auctions scheduled. She was seriously considering it today as a matter of fact. But Danny and his wife, Barb, were expecting their first child any day now, and she figured he was feeling the pressure to get a "real" job. She had a feeling their days of doing what they both loved were dwindling fast.

Cass and Danny had been willed the property they lived on, a non-working farm close to the county line, when their father died two years ago. She'd been living in the cabin for more than a decade, but it was originally built for her grandmother who refused to live there. She knew Cass's father only constructed the place so he could control her, as he did everyone else in his life. To say Cass felt no sorrow at his passing was putting it mildly.

The cabin stood on a plot of land that had held a small barn for housing horses when the farm was thriving, that had been long before her father purchased it. When her parents bought the place, they restructured the land and sold off part of the acreage to local farmers who wanted the fields to raise their crops. Other sections of the land were being rented for the same purpose, and the money they now received for that was split three ways between herself, Danny, and their mother, Sara.

She glanced around the interior of the cabin after Gordy was done outside and felt a contentment she didn't usually allow herself. It was a large open space with a staircase leading to a loft, where her bedroom was, from the far side of the room next to the kitchen. This was home. And at least this space didn't hold any bad memories of her childhood, unlike the main house where Danny and Barb lived. Cass had been more than happy to let them have the house while she gladly stayed in the cabin. She had everything she needed right here. Running water, an indoor toilet, and a place to sleep. What else could she ask for? The fact the property had been completely paid off before her father died was a bonus. Cass was able to live on the property for just the cost of half the yearly taxes.

She felt her phone vibrate against her hip and fought to get her hand inside her snow pants to retrieve it before she missed the call. Of course it was Danny. Who else would it be at the ass-crack of dawn?

"I'm not lying when I tell you there's a big part of me hoping today's auctions have been cancelled," she said.

"No such luck," he answered with a laugh. "Although the first location is down to one unit, so I say we skip it and just head to the second facility. That'll give us a little extra time to get there in case the roads are a total mess. And maybe we can get there before the rest of the caravan, because it's a bitch trying to park the truck even when there aren't six-foot-high snow drifts."

"Sounds good. I'll be there in a few." Cass hung up and went to the fridge to get the big bottle of water she always took with her. When she turned to head back to the door, she almost tripped over Gordy. She crouched down and looked him in the eye. "You're going to be a good boy while Mommy's out working today, right? I can't afford to buy new pillows every time I leave you alone."

He cocked his head to the side as though he understood her. She'd gotten him from a shelter where his owners had abandoned him because he had separation anxiety. He'd been better since she realized if she left the television or the radio on while she was gone he didn't seem to be as stressed out. They'd started to find their groove before the auctions stopped back in November. She hoped he hadn't regressed since she'd been home with him so much over the winter.

She smiled at the memory of the mess she'd walked in on the first time she'd left him alone. She liked to sleep with a lot of pillows on her bed, and he'd ripped every single one of them apart. There'd been stuffing and feathers strewn all over the cabin. The pillow shredding incident happened almost a year ago, and she was still finding the stray feather every once in a while. Needless to say, it had been the last time she used feather pillows.

Cass patted him on the head and kissed his snout before heading out to make her way to the main house. Barb was waiting in the doorway for her, a big cup of coffee in her hand and a smile on her face. Cass took the coffee and kissed her on the cheek.

"If you weren't straight, I'd marry you in a heartbeat," Cass said with a grin.

"Liar," Barb answered with a laugh. She took Cass's hand and placed it on her belly. "Your nephew's been kicking up a storm since three o'clock this morning."

Cass looked at her in wonder as she felt a little foot bounce against her hand. It was amazing to think a tiny human life was growing inside there. Cass was just happy it was someone else. She had no desire to procreate. In fact, small children scared the hell out of her. She was still trying to figure out how to tell Barb her built-in babysitter wasn't going to do much good if she was hiding in the closet every time the baby cried.

"Where's my brother?" she asked before ushering Barb inside. Standing in the cold couldn't be good for her in her condition, right?

"He's in the shower." Barb led her into the kitchen and motioned for her to have a seat. "Are pancakes all right for breakfast?"

"You don't have to feed me." The response was merely habit for Cass. Barb made pancakes almost every morning, and Cass was usually there to eat them.

"Please. If I don't, who will? Of course, if you'd find a nice woman to settle down with, maybe I wouldn't have to worry about whether or not you're eating."

"Pancakes are fine." Cass didn't want to go there. She folded her arms across her chest, her way of telling the world to go away. Her heart ached at the thought of how her mother had given up her dreams to marry her father in order to raise her and Danny. There was no way she was going to make the same mistake. Settling down wasn't part of her agenda. Never had been and never would be.

"Have you heard from her lately?" Barb asked, seeming to read her mind.

"She called the other night from Okinawa." Cass was happy her mother was finally able to do the things she wanted to do, instead of what her husband told her—or forced her—to do. She'd always wanted to travel, and she was making the most of life now that she was in her fifties. Cass wanted to enjoy life while she was still young, not when she might be too old or too frail to do it later on.

Danny had been furious when they'd found out their father left everything to them, and nothing for their mother. But their mother had been ecstatic to not get the property upon his death. She'd hated it there. Cass always thought she belonged in the city, not in the middle of nowhere otherwise known as western New York. And now she was. Traveling all over the world and visiting every city she possibly could. Although Cass was fairly certain she was going to settle down in Japan. She seemed to be completely enthralled with the place.

"She seems happy?" Barb asked as she put a plate in front of Cass and sat across from her. The breath she sucked in as she winced in obvious pain worried Cass.

"What's wrong?" she asked, rushing to kneel beside her, one hand on Barb's knee. Barb covered her hand with her own and breathed in through her nose.

"This little bugger kicks hard," she said with a forced laugh.

"Bullshit," Cass stood and looked over her shoulder for Danny. Where the hell was he? She'd heard the water shut off ten minutes ago. "You're having a contraction, aren't you?"

"No." The way Barb clutched the table so hard her knuckles turned white was all Cass needed to let her know Barb was lying.

"Jesus, you're due any day. Does Danny know? How far apart are they?"

"Calm down, Cass. It's not a contraction, and I'm hardly due any day. He isn't supposed to come for three more weeks." Barb closed her eyes, and Cass watched as she tried to control her breathing. "Have you forgotten I'm a doctor?"

"A general surgeon is hardly an OB/GYN, Barb."

"You worry too much. There's plenty of time before he makes his debut into the world."

"Like father, like son. I'm guessing Danny never told you he was born an entire month early." Cass didn't know what the hell to do. She headed for the living room but stopped and looked back at Barb. "Don't move. I'm going to find him."

She ran up the stairs and barged right into the master bedroom without knocking. She turned her back quickly when she saw Danny standing there in nothing but his birthday suit. He let out a yell and covered himself with his hands before she registered what she was seeing.

"Christ, Cass, don't you know how to knock?"

"Like I haven't seen you naked before."

"Yeah, when I was like six. What the hell are you doing here?"

"Your wife is in labor."

"Now?"

"Yes, now," Cass said, exasperated. She turned around to face him, hoping she'd given him enough time to at least get his underwear on. She breathed a sigh of relief to see him zipping up his pants. That was a visual she never wanted to see again. "You need to get her to the hospital."

"But we have auctions to go to."

"Are you serious? You think an auction's more important than your first child being born? You aren't going anywhere but with your wife to the hospital. Finish getting dressed, for God's sake."

Cass hung around just long enough to make sure they got out of the driveway safely before getting in the box truck and heading for Buffalo.

Chapter Two

"Hey, Cassidy!"

Cass ignored the man calling her name. Rodney gave her a serious case of the creeps. She and Danny joked about how he probably only showered once a year. Religiously. It was bad enough dealing with his snide remarks when Danny was there with her, but today she'd have to handle him alone. She hoped she'd be able to refrain from punching him right in the nose the first time he made a lewd comment.

She made her way inside the office to register for a number and thanked the clerk when he handed it over to her. Once back outside, she scanned the crowd quickly but didn't see Rodney. She took a deep breath and relaxed slightly. But then the stench reached her nostrils and she turned to see him standing behind her, his grin revealing the gaps in his yellow teeth.

"Where's your brother today?"

"His wife is having a baby so I'm on my own today."

"He's letting you do this on your own? He's a braver man than me."

"What the hell is that supposed to mean?" she asked, knowing she shouldn't let him get to her, but damn, he was nasty.

"Calm down, honey." He laughed, which only pissed her off more. "I know how women are, that's all. You're liable to see a pretty handbag or a nice piece of furniture and overbid."

"Because I look like the type to drool over a pretty handbag, right?"

"You're a woman, ain't you?"

"Your powers of deduction are astounding, Rodney." She started to walk away but turned back to him, unable to help herself. She lowered her voice so the woman a few feet away from them with a small child couldn't hear her. "Stay the fuck away from me, do you understand? Just because I'm a woman doesn't mean I like frilly things. I do, however, like the women who like frilly things."

She was satisfied by the bewildered look on his face, and she couldn't help the laugh at his expense. No doubt it would take him a while to fully realize what she'd just told him. She prayed he'd leave her alone while he tried to figure it out.

She moved a few feet away from him and took in the crowd of people before her. It used to be only a handful of bidders before those damn television shows made everyone think they could get rich buying storage units at auction. The truth was, you were more likely to lose money than make much of a profit, but every once in a great while you'd find a unit that paid off big. It was why she continued to do it. Taking a gamble was necessary sometimes in her line of work.

The trick was knowing what to look for. Some bidders liked to bid on what they couldn't see, but she and Danny stuck to the idea of only bidding on what you *could* see. That didn't always mean you could actually see something of value. It meant if the units were clean—neatly packed and full of obviously well taken care of items—they would probably bid on it. On the other hand, if it looked like things were just thrown in there in a hurry, they weren't too interested.

"Rodney bothering you again?"

Cass turned to see an older couple walking up to her. Tom and Maggie were good people. They'd befriended her and Danny a couple of years prior when she and Danny had helped them clean out a particularly bad unit. It had been literally full of garbage. Junk mail, old prescription bottles, and clothes that had definitely seen better days. What little furniture there had been was broken and not worth trying to repair.

"Hey, Tom, it's good to see you again," she said as she hugged him briefly before turning to his wife and doing the same. "Maggie, you look as beautiful as ever."

"As do you," Maggie replied with a slight blush to her cheeks.

"Where's Danny?" Tom asked. "He usually keeps Rodney in line."

"Barb went into labor this morning," Cass explained. "But if push came to shove, I'm sure I could handle Rodney on my own."

"I have no doubt." Tom laughed as he looked over at the man in question. He shook his head in disgust and turned back to them. "Tell Danny congratulations for us."

"Will do." Cass saw the auctioneer heading for the gate, and the crowd moved forward in anticipation. Cass had hoped the influx of people curious to see how the whole process worked would thin out over time, but it didn't seem to be happening. For the most part they were only there to observe, but there were always a few intent on driving up the prices.

Cass hung back as the first unit was opened. She preferred to let everyone else look first so she could hear what comments were being made. You never knew when someone else might see something you didn't. Rodney was notorious for pointing out things to his business partner other people failed to notice.

The first three lockers were crap, as far as Cass could tell, and they'd gone for way too much money. The fourth one held a little promise though. There was an antique dining room set she was sure most of the bidders present had no desire to move. But if the people who owned it had money for a set so obviously expensive and well kept, then she was sure they had other things of value in there. Yes, the furniture was big, and most definitely heavy, but there was real potential in this unit.

She set an amount of seven hundred dollars for the unit, figuring she'd be able to get at least that much only for what she could see. She just hoped she was right about nobody wanting to deal with it. And she trusted Danny would be available to help her clean it all out by the end of the week.

The auctioneer was looking for a starting bid of five hundred, but nobody was biting. She saw a few people shaking their heads and turning away. When he dropped all the way down to one hundred, Cass gave him a nod. She felt her heartrate speed up when somebody raised their hand for one fifty. She'd never seen this particular guy before, but he obviously had more money than brains based on how much he'd paid for the first unit. Cass nodded again for two hundred.

"Three hundred!" Rodney yelled just as the bidding was about to close. He gave her a wink and a smile that made her skin crawl.

"Four hundred," Cass said calmly. Mr. More-dollars-than-sense shook his head, looking for all the world like she was hurting his feelings by bidding against him. Cass hoped nobody else would jump in and Rodney would think she might drop the unit on him if he tried to raise it much further. She knew there was no way in hell he was going to move all the furniture on his own since his partner wasn't there either.

Cass grinned to herself when the bidding ended there, and she went to place a padlock on the door to secure her winnings.

"Good buy," the auctioneer said to her.

"You aren't going to look through it?" Rodney asked as everyone else dispersed since the auction was done. They only had twenty minutes to get to the next stop on the all day caravan.

"Nope." Cass checked to make sure the lock was secured then began walking toward the office so she could pay for the unit. She sped up when she heard him following her. He had to be about four hundred pounds, and she was surprised he was managing to keep up with her. He was breathing heavily and obviously struggling, but damn if he wasn't right on her tail.

"So, you're a dyke?" he said just before she reached the office.

"I'm a lesbian, yes," she answered, readying herself for a confrontation.

"That's cool," he said, much to her amazement. "My ex-wife is a dyke too."

"What a surprise," Cass muttered under her breath. Then, before she could stop herself, "Wait, someone actually married you?"

He laughed, but she could see the pain in his eyes. Great, now she felt bad. She'd hurt his feelings, and he was trying to play it off like it was no big deal.

"I know, crazy, right?"

"I'm sorry," she said, and she meant it. No matter how much this guy gave her the willies, there'd been no reason for the insensitive comment.

"Don't be," he told her. "Sometimes I have the same thought."

As he walked away, she let her head drop in shame. After a few seconds, she chuckled. Danny was going to get a kick out of it when she told him later.

❖

Cass bought two more units later in the day. They'd been relatively small, so she was able to clean them out herself. She'd returned home and was in the back of the truck sorting through things and unloading into the garage they used as a warehouse when Danny pulled into the driveway.

"How's my nephew?" she called when he got out of the car.

"Refusing to leave the warmth of his mother's womb," Danny answered with an exhausted sigh. "I can't say I blame him though. I wouldn't want to be thrust into this frigid weather either."

"Damn, she's still in labor?"

"They told me it would still be a few hours so I should come home and get some rest." He climbed into the truck with her and opened a box. "Did you get anything good?"

"There's some tools over there, and a flat screen TV I haven't tested yet. It's in the garage. Otherwise, it's just a bunch of crap as far as I can tell."

"Was this all you got?"

"No, there's a unit with antique furniture. I didn't get a chance to look at anything in it though. I figured I'd go back tomorrow and see what I can see."

"If the baby comes overnight, I'll come with you."

"Don't worry about it. We have until Monday morning to clean it out," she said. She stood and rubbed her hands together briskly before putting her gloves back on.

"Come inside and have something hot to drink," Danny said as he jumped down to the ground. "I'll make some soup or something."

He didn't need to ask her twice. She'd only been out there twenty minutes, but she was feeling like an ice cube already. She hated the hot weather almost as much as the cold, but she was certainly looking forward to spring.

CHAPTER THREE

"I'll see you tomorrow, Trish," Erica Jacobs said at the time clock. As soon as it changed to two thirty, she swiped her card. The first few days of her new job in a new town hadn't been as bad as she'd thought it would be. Of course she knew now why it had seemed so easy to get this position. Nobody from the bigger cities wanted to be working in a small office where a rush was two people waiting on line to mail a package.

Lucky for her, she'd wanted to get away from Syracuse. Here, she was close enough for her little brother since it was only a two-hour drive, but far enough away she wouldn't run the risk of seeing her parents in random places at random times. They'd disowned her when she'd finally found the courage to come out to them two years earlier.

Not having a tough time coming to grips with it, but actually *disowned* her. As in they refused to speak to her, and they refused to allow her to have any contact with her brother, Kyle. In fact, she was pretty sure they even refused to admit they had a daughter any longer.

Kyle would be turning sixteen in less than two months, and he'd confided in her about his own sexuality. Erica was pretty sure she'd talked him out of telling their parents until he was at least done with high school, because she couldn't imagine what might happen to him if they decided to kick him out of the house when he was still so young.

Kyle had been a surprise baby. Erica was fourteen when he was born and had always been his protector. Of course, back then they'd been one big happy family. She shook her head at the utter lack of fairness in life.

"Hey, Erica," Trish called right before she walked out the door.

"Yeah?"

"Eddie and I are going for drinks when I'm done here tonight," Trish said. Eddie was their rural carrier who had a huge crush on the very married Trish. "Please say you'll come with us. I only agreed to it because Vince is out of town on business. I like Eddie, but he can't seem to get it through his mind I'm not available. You'd be doing me a huge favor if you could be there to run interference for me."

Erica started to say she couldn't make it, but realized there was really no reason she couldn't. It wasn't like she had a lot of options her first weekend in town. Laundry was a lame excuse, and she was sure Trish would see through the lie. She shrugged in defeat.

"Sure, why not?"

"Thank you, thank you, thank you," Trish said as she grabbed her forearm and squeezed. The relief was obvious in her eyes. "Seven?"

Erica agreed and got the details about where they were going and how to get there. If it wasn't on her short commute from her mobile home to the post office, she had no clue where anything was. She hadn't even been to a grocery store yet, and she was definitely going to have to remedy that dilemma soon. Surviving on McDonald's was quickly losing its appeal if it even held any to begin with, which honestly it hadn't.

She was patting herself on the back for having the foresight to invest in a GPS before moving out to the sticks. The village of Dallas, New York, where Erica lived and worked, was in Orleans County, and the closest town of any size was Batavia, but even that was a good thirty-minute drive. Trish said they were having drinks somewhere in a town called Elba, which was where Trish lived, but was still quite a drive for Erica. According to the GPS, Elba was only a few minutes closer to her than Batavia.

The trailer park Erica lived in was nice enough, especially compared to some she'd encountered while searching for a place to live. She just never thought she'd ever be living in a mobile home. Correction, *manufactured* home. Not that she was a snob or anything, but her limited experience with trailer parks had left a bad taste in her mouth. Nope, she wasn't going to go there. Those memories were better left tucked away in the far corners of her mind.

She opened the door to her house and was greeted by Willie, her orange tabby with an attitude the size of Texas. He wove his way through her legs and looked up at her with an insistent meow before sauntering off to the kitchen. Apparently, his inner clock was telling him it was time for dinner. Erica knew better than to ignore him. If she did, he'd plant himself on her lap and stare at her until she finally gave in. It was freaky the way he'd stare sometimes.

Once he was fed, she sat at her kitchen table and opened her laptop. After a quick look at her email, she sighed. There was another message from Kyle. He'd sent at least one every day since she'd left, all of them begging her to let him come live with her. She knew the only reason he was miserable was because he hated lying to their parents. He'd always talked to them about everything, as she had when she was younger, but telling them he was gay wasn't something they would handle well. She knew it for a fact, and so did he.

She fired off a hasty note imploring him once again to wait it out until he graduated. She hated that the only way she was able to communicate with him was through his best friend's email account, but he'd told her their father was checking his computer daily. They really didn't want him to have any contact with her.

Like he could catch being gay.

Erica chuckled at the thought, because she was certain it was exactly what they would think when he did finally come out to them.

She made a light lunch and threw a load of clothes in the wash. Huh, she really could have used the need to do laundry as an excuse to not go out with Trish and Eddie. Who knew? She considered watching some television, but if she was having drinks tonight, she'd probably need a nap. Her work schedule had her going to bed no later than eight o'clock and getting up at four in the morning in order to start work at six. She was still getting used to the odd hours, but it wasn't as bad as she thought it might be.

Unless she happened to find someone she wanted to date. Who in their right mind would want to date a thirty-year-old woman who had an eight o'clock curfew on a work night? It was going to make meeting other lesbians difficult, she was sure. But maybe it would be for the best. She had a habit of falling too quickly for women, and she blamed her parents. She'd been so happy growing up, and she wanted to have a relationship like they had. They were so obviously in love, and totally devoted to each other. It was supposed to be that way, right? But she thought you were always supposed to love and support your children as well.

She got into bed and pulled the covers up over her head so Willie wouldn't lick her hair and wake her up. He was such a strange cat, but she loved him. As she drifted off to sleep, she had a fleeting thought. Maybe she needed to take a break from dating. Or at least keep things slow if she met a woman she really liked.

Yeah, right. Like that was going to happen.

❖

Erica was seriously considering leaving the bar when she saw it was nine o'clock. Eddie seemed to finally be getting the hint Trish wasn't interested, and damn it, Erica was tired. And it wasn't like this was a real happening place. There were three people at the bar, and only two of the dozen tables in the room were occupied, theirs being one of them. Eddie was playing pool with some guy in the far corner of the room.

Welcome to Friday night in Middle-of-Nowhere, New York.

"Thanks for coming tonight, Erica," Trish said as she stood and put her coat on. "I've got to be getting home because Vince usually calls around ten. See you Tuesday."

Erica didn't know what to say. Wasn't it rude to ask someone to go for drinks and just up and leave? She held up her beer bottle and saw it was still more than half full. She took a swig from it and decided she'd only stay until it was gone.

She looked up when the front door opened and a couple of loud people came in. In fact, every head in the place turned toward them as they entered.

"Jim!" said the woman as though she were in a New York City dance club and had to yell in order to be heard over the music. "I'm buying a round for the house. My baby brother here just became a daddy."

"Congratulations, Danny!" came the cry from everyone present, except for Erica.

She didn't know any of these people, and she hoped she could sneak out before anyone noticed. No such luck. She was slipping her coat on when the woman appeared at her table holding two bottles of beer. And damn it, it was the brand she was drinking. The woman placed one of the bottles on the table in front of Erica.

"You aren't leaving, are you?" she asked with a lopsided smile Erica was sure made most people melt. Men or women. "The party's just getting started."

Without taking her coat off, Erica slid back into the chair. She couldn't stop herself. She'd started to think all the women around here were either old or married, or both. Of course, she didn't know if this one was married or not, but there was no ring, which was a good sign, and she definitely wasn't old.

"The name's Cassidy Holmes, but you can call me Cass," she said, holding her hand out.

"Erica," she managed as she took it. She couldn't help thinking Cass held her hand a little longer than was necessary, but it felt nice.

"I haven't seen you around here before."

"How original," Erica said with a roll of her eyes. She felt a flutter in her chest when a look of amusement flashed in Cass's light brown eyes. Erica watched in silent fascination as Cass ran a hand absently through her dark brown hair. She was sexy as hell, and Erica got the impression she was well aware of the fact.

"It's not a line," Cass said, leaning across the table and speaking quietly. "Unless you want it to be?"

Erica stifled a laugh. Like Cass would want her, an out-of-shape postal worker. Of course, it wasn't as though there were a lot of lesbians around to choose from. She took a drink of her beer because she was afraid she might say something stupid. Beautiful women didn't talk to her. It just didn't happen.

"All I meant was I really haven't seen you before," Cass said, relaxing into her chair. She shrugged and glanced back at the bar where her brother was passing out cigars. "And you know how small towns are. Everybody knows everybody. So, are you just passing through?"

"Hey, Cass," said Eddie as he arrived at their table. He pulled his jacket off the back of a chair and slipped it on. "How's business?"

"Pretty much nonexistent through the winter, but I went to a few auctions earlier today, and I'm optimistic."

"Glad to hear it," he said before turning to Erica. "I'll see you at work, yeah?"

She nodded her response and was surprised to see the smile Cass didn't even try to hide. Once Eddie was gone, Erica decided to steer the conversation away from where she worked.

"So, you became an aunt today. First time?"

"Actually, yeah." The look on Cass's face was wistful, almost as though she was realizing it for the first time herself. "I am. I mean, I've been referring to him as my nephew ever since they found out the sex, but I don't think it hit me until you said it just now. I'm an aunt."

"Why do I get the feeling the thought of it scares you?"

"Probably because it does."

"Why?"

Cass began peeling the label off her beer bottle, contemplating the question. She glanced up and met Erica's eyes. The thought flitting through her mind brought her up short. *I could get lost in those eyes.* They were such a bright blue, even in the dark bar. Cass had never seen eyes so blue in her life. And the blond hair held back in a ponytail was sexy, but she was sure Erica had no clue. She brought her mind back to the question Erica was waiting on an answer for and blew out a breath.

"They're going to want me to babysit. Don't people expect as much from their siblings when they have a baby?" Cass shook her head but never broke eye contact. "I am so not that person."

"What do you mean?" Erica seemed appalled at the notion. "You won't babysit your own nephew?"

"Small children frighten me." Jesus, she'd never admitted that to anyone before. "I mean, what if I drop him or something?"

"Hey, what's happening?" Danny asked as he handed her a cigar. He offered one to Erica, but she shook her head.

"Congratulations on becoming a father," Erica said with a smile.

"Thanks. I'm Danny."

"Erica."

Danny smiled as he looked back and forth between them. He wouldn't be happy until Cass settled down and had a family of her own. Not happening. Ever. When he turned to her and raised an eyebrow in question as he tilted his head toward Erica, Cass shook her head.

"Cass was just telling me how she can't wait to babysit so you and your wife can go out to dinner and a movie. You know, enjoy some time alone."

Cass looked at her in disbelief. What the hell was she doing? Erica refused to look at her and was smiling sweetly at Danny. When he looked at her she was too dumbstruck to do anything but stare. She was sure she resembled a deer in headlights.

"Really? I had the impression she was dreading it. Thanks, sis. I can't wait to tell Barb the good news. And to think, she wasn't even going to ask you to babysit."

He walked away then, and Cass glared at Erica until she finally met her eyes, a pleased look on her face.

"What the hell did you just do?"

"You need to babysit your nephew."

"Then you're helping." Cass smiled at the idea forming in her mind. Erica laughed and shook her head. "You owe me. You threw me under the damn bus. I can't believe you just did that. You can't deny you owe me."

"Fine. If you ever agree to babysit, I'll give you my phone number so you can call me for advice."

Cass watched as Erica got up and walked out the door without another word. Cass liked her. She was so much more interesting than the women she met at the bars in either Buffalo or Rochester. But those other women she never had to see again. Eddie's comment made it apparent Erica was the new window clerk at the post office in Dallas, and Cass would therefore be seeing a lot more of her. Hooking up with her was a bad idea. Even though she was the sexiest woman Cass had met in a long time.

No, she thought as she downed the last of her beer, Erica was off-limits.

Damn it.

Chapter Four

Cass thanked Trish for holding the door open so she could maneuver her hand truck inside the post office. Selling things online was a pain in the ass, but she couldn't deny how totally awesome it felt when someone purchased something out of the blue she'd had listed for months and more than likely forgot about. She was shipping three boxes today, but once the storage auctions were in full swing, she'd probably have three times as many going out every day.

She made her way to the window and placed the first box on the counter before realizing no one was there to wait on her. She glanced back and saw Trish emptying the blue box out front, so she rang the bell to get someone's attention. It took a few seconds, but Erica finally emerged from the back. Cass couldn't help the smile when their eyes met and Erica's step faltered ever so slightly.

"Hello again," she said, trying her best to act nonchalant and hide the fact she found Erica attractive. "Fancy meeting you here."

"I'm sorry, do I know you?" Erica took the first package from her and set it on the scale, but Cass saw the grin she was trying to hide.

"So this is how you want to play it?" Cass asked with an amused grin. "Hard to get? I don't mind. I like a challenge."

"What makes you think you can get me at all?" Erica asked, finally meeting Cass's gaze.

"The look in your eye right now. It's the same look you gave me Friday night in the bar." Cass grabbed the second package and set it on the counter. The next words out of her mouth surprised even her. "Have dinner with me."

"Excuse me?"

Erica was looking at her as though she'd lost her mind, and maybe she had. She reminded herself Erica was a local, and therefore off-limits. In fact, anyone she might run into at the local grocery store was off-limits.

"I would like to take you out to dinner." She had the feeling Erica was going to turn her down, and now her ego was ruling her thought process. Women didn't often turn her down, but when they did, Cass treated the rejection as a test of her willingness to pursue.

"I don't think so," Erica said, turning her attention back to her job. "Anything liquid, fragile, or perishable?"

"No," Cass answered. "Why do you not think so?"

Erica questioned her about how she wanted to ship the packages, reciting the prices displayed by the credit card machine on the counter in front of Cass. They only talked about the shipments until Erica finished the last package.

"Just so you know," Cass said, leaning across the counter so she wouldn't have to speak too loudly. "When I see something I like, I don't give up. Are you sure you won't have dinner with me sometime?"

"It would be a bad idea, Cass."

"No, it wouldn't."

"It would," Erica said with a sad smile. "Why are you wasting your time trying to get me to go out with you when you could have anyone you want? I mean, let's face it. I'm no prize in the looks department."

"Are you serious?" Cass was stunned at the declaration. She heard Trish coming back inside so she waited for her to disappear into the back. "Erica, I don't know what you see in the mirror, but I see a beautiful woman standing before me."

"I'm overweight and out of shape."

"Who isn't?" Cass took a step away from the counter and grabbed her hand truck. She certainly hadn't planned on asking Erica to dinner, but she'd done so because she was attracted to her. It was ridiculous to her that Erica would see herself in a negative light. Before she left she gave Erica a long look. "You don't even know me. I'm sorry the impression you have of me is someone who's so shallow."

She turned and walked out of the building without looking back, even though she heard Erica calling her name. If Erica thought so little of her, why should she waste her time?

❖

Erica wanted to go after her, but she knew by the time she got outside, Cass would probably be long gone. The look on her face as she'd delivered her final words had pulled at something deep inside Erica. She felt the overwhelming desire to protect Cass, but from what, exactly? Like she'd said, Erica didn't even know her.

But she wanted to.

The thought startled her. If it was true, then why had she said no to Cass's offer of dinner? She should have said yes, wanted to say yes, but it was a bad idea. If they got along, Erica wasn't sure she could force herself to take things slow. She had a tendency to rush into things where women were concerned. She'd always become lovers without even knowing if she liked the other woman. It was time to slow things down and become friends with a woman before jumping into bed with her. The only problem? Cassidy Holmes was all kinds of sexy.

"Hey, are you all right?" Trish asked, breaking her out of her thoughts.

"I'm fine," she answered, forcing a smile.

"Did Cass say something to upset you?"

"Why would you think that?"

"Because she's a flirt. Don't get me wrong, she's a great person, the type who would give you the shirt off her back if you needed it, but she flirts with everyone. Do you want me to tell her to back off?"

"I'm a big girl, Trish. I can handle it."

"Are you…I mean…"

Erica could tell by the way Trish shifted her weight from one leg to the other and kept looking away what she was trying to ask. She thought it might be fun to let her squirm for a few minutes. Erica didn't usually come out to just anyone, but she'd never lie if anyone came right out and asked if she was gay.

"Am I what?" Trish's cheeks reddened and she looked like she wanted to be anywhere but there, having this particular conversation. Erica decided to give her a break. "A lesbian?"

"Yeah."

"Would it make a difference if I was?"

"Not to me," Trish said with conviction. "But there are a lot of people who think it's wrong. Just because the Supreme Court ruled same-sex marriage is legal doesn't mean everyone agrees with it."

"Trust me, I know," Erica said, her father's angry face flashing through her memory banks. "And yes, I am a lesbian."

"Then maybe you should give Cass a chance. I don't think I've ever seen her so dejected as she looked when she walked out of here."

"Maybe I will," she answered thoughtfully.

She couldn't shake the feeling that this was so not a good idea.

Chapter Five

Cass was on her way home from Batavia after selling some scrap gold and silver she'd found in the storage unit with all the antique furniture when she saw a group of four kids in a field alongside the road. She was going to just keep on going until she saw one of them knock another boy down, and then they all started kicking and punching the boy.

She pulled over to the side of the road and grabbed the baseball bat she kept in the backseat for protection before running into the field. It was no easy feat with the snow so deep, but she somehow managed. None of them saw her coming because they were too intent on beating the shit out of the kid they'd knocked down. They were laughing and taunting him, and it took everything she had in her to not swing the bat at their heads. Instead, she grabbed the closest one by the collar of his jacket and pulled him backward, causing him to land on his ass.

"What the fuck?" he said as he looked up at her. When he saw the bat cocked above her shoulder, he hurried to cover his head with his arms.

Cass looked back in time to see the other two kids running off toward the road. Just as she thought. Cowards. The boy they'd been attacking was still lying on his side in the fetal position, his arms also covering his head.

"You okay?" she asked him from where she was standing, keeping the bat raised so the kid on the ground wouldn't get any stupid ideas. There was blood in the snow near where his head was, but it didn't appear to be enough to cause any real concern.

She watched as he slowly uncovered his head and looked around to make sure his assailants were really gone. He then turned his eyes to her and she saw he looked totally pissed off.

"Who the hell are you?"

Cass didn't answer, but glanced at the kid she'd knocked on his ass to make sure he wasn't planning an attack on her. He was still exactly where she'd left him, but now he was crying. She felt absolutely no sympathy for the guy. Her mother had always told her if you stood up to a bully, they'd run away with their tail between their legs. She'd never truly believed it until now.

"I'm the one who just saved your sorry ass, so how about a little gratitude?" she asked when she looked back at him as he was getting to his feet.

"I didn't ask for your help." The kid definitely had attitude, but she suspected it was for the other boy's benefit. He didn't want to let on how scared he really was. She couldn't blame him. If she hadn't come along when she did, they might have very well killed him, because they hadn't looked like they were going to stop beating him anytime soon.

"Sorry. Not how it looked from where I was sitting." She turned her body so she could keep an eye on both boys and finally let the bat rest against her shoulder. She didn't allow herself to completely relax though. Who knew what the dynamic between this set of boys was? The one they were beating could be part of their group, and they could both turn on her if she were to let her guard down. "Why were they beating you up?"

"Are you a cop?" he asked and touched a finger to the corner of his mouth. When he pulled it away and saw blood, he wiped it on his pants that were wet from the snow.

Cass rolled her eyes and pushed the other kid's leg with her foot. He shied away as though he expected the bat to connect with his head any second.

"Why were you guys attacking him?"

"He's a faggot," the kid said, sounding like he was finally finding his courage again. Cass tightened her grip on the bat just in case. He pulled his arms away from his head and looked up at her, his eyes full of defiance. "If you're here to save him, you must be a dyke."

"I'm not sure I follow your reasoning, but before you decide to get all cocky and shit," she said with a smile, "you might want to take a look around. Your buddies are long gone. Probably ran all the way home crying to their mommas."

"You don't scare me, bitch," he said as he got to his feet.

"You sure about that?" Cass gripped the bat like she was going to swing it and took a step toward him. She shook her head and let out a nervous laugh when he turned and ran off. After a moment, she went back to the other kid. "Are you all right?"

"I'm fine." He jerked away from her when she reached out to touch his jaw.

"What's your name?"

"Kyle."

"Kyle what?" she asked when it became obvious he didn't intend to give her a last name.

"Jacobs."

"Okay, Kyle Jacobs, where do you live?"

"Dallas," he said after thinking about it for a minute.

"Dallas? In Orleans County?" Cass asked. Kyle shrugged and nodded. "Is that a yes, or an I don't know?"

"I don't know what county it's in," he finally admitted, suddenly finding something immensely interesting at his feet. "It's north of here, and this road runs through it."

"Do you drive?" Kyle shook his head in response and Cass sighed. It was more difficult getting information out of this kid than she thought it should be. "Then what the hell are you doing in Elba?"

"Walking."

"Smartass. Come on, I'm taking you home." She grabbed him by the arm, but he pulled away from her. He was a big kid, probably close to six feet, and Cass knew she should probably be wary of him, but she had a gut feeling he wasn't a threat to her.

"I'm not getting in your car. You think I'm stupid?"

She was seriously beginning to wonder, but she simply shook her head. She sighed and opened her arms toward him, looking down at herself.

"Do I look like a kidnapper?"

"You were going to hit that kid with your bat," he said, and she thought she saw the ghost of a smile. He used a hand to brush his blond hair away from his eyes. "Maybe you're a serial killer. Maybe you want to kill me."

"I wanted to kill him because he was attacking you, but I didn't," she pointed out. "I just want to get you home so your parents don't worry about you."

He hesitated as if he were considering his options. Maybe it was because they were a good twenty minutes by car from Dallas, or maybe his reasons were something else entirely, but he finally nodded and followed her back to her car. She got him to give her an address before she pulled out onto the road.

"Are you a lesbian?" he asked after they'd been driving for ten minutes or so. He didn't look at her though. He just stared out the window.

"I'm not sure my sexuality is any of your business." Cass wondered if she should be honest with him. Maybe he was gay and was looking for someone to connect with. "You didn't know those kids, did you?"

"No."

"Why were they beating you up?"

"Like he said, because I'm gay. Because the one you almost made shit his pants was pretending he was interested in me, and I took the bait."

"How old are you?"

"Sixteen," he answered and looked at her. "*Almost* sixteen. But before you tell me I'm too young to know I'm gay—"

"Whoa, totally not why I was asking, all right?" She glanced at him out of the corner of her eye and saw a scared kid. Obviously, his adrenaline had faded and he realized what had happened. "I knew I was a lesbian when I was like five, okay? I'm not going to judge you."

"Really?"

"Yeah." Cass looked at the street signs and found the one he said he lived on. She turned and went slowly down the road in the trailer park until she found the address he'd given her. "You stay here, all right? I want to talk to your parents."

He looked nervous but nodded, and she got out of the car. She didn't know what to expect. He hadn't told her why he was so far from home. What if his parents were abusive, and he ran away to escape them? He was carrying a backpack, and it appeared as though it might bust at the seams. She went up the steps to the front door and glanced back at the car before ringing the bell.

She ran a quick scenario through her head, working out what she was going to say to his parents. *I found some kids beating the crap out of your son.* She shook her head. Too insensitive. None of it mattered though, when the door opened.

"Cass?" Erica asked, looking as surprised as Cass felt. "What are you doing here? How did you know where I lived?"

"I didn't." She shook her head, and damn it all, she couldn't form any other words. She glanced back at her car and saw Kyle watching her. What the hell? Was Erica his mother? "Maybe he gave me the wrong address."

"Who?"

"Do you have a son?" Cass focused her attention on Erica, who looked to be truly perplexed.

"No," she said slowly. "What's going on?"

"I saw some kids beating the crap out of him, and I stopped to help." Cass shifted her weight from one foot to the other. He had to have given her the wrong address. What other explanation could there possibly be? Cass took a deep breath before meeting Erica's gaze. "When I told him I was going to drive him home, he said this was where he lived."

"What's his name?" Erica looked worried now, and it only caused Cass to wonder what was really going on here. "How old is he?"

"Fifteen. He told me his name is Kyle." Cass watched as Erica's facial features morphed from confusion to concern in less than a few seconds.

"Son of a bitch," Erica said as she pushed past Cass and walked quickly to the passenger door of Cass's car. She didn't hesitate to whip the door open and grab Kyle by the collar, pulling him out of the passenger seat. "What the hell are you doing here? Do Mom and Dad know you're gone?"

"I ran away."

"You *what*?" she asked. This was so not a good situation. Now she was going to have to call them, and she doubted they wanted to speak to her any more than she wanted to talk to them. She took him by the arm and led him into the house, almost running into Cass along the way. She met her eyes after she shoved Kyle inside. "I'm sorry. Please come in. Kyle's my little brother."

"I should go," Cass answered. "I'll talk to you later, okay?"

"Please? I want you to come inside. You said you saved him from being beat up, but he's bleeding." Erica looked in the house and saw Kyle sitting on the couch, dried blood all over his face. And he kept placing a hand over his ribs. "I could use your help cleaning him up while I call our parents."

"Sure," Cass said, sounding reluctant but following her in.

Erica directed them to the bathroom and let out an exasperated breath before grabbing her cell phone from the coffee table and dialing the number she still knew by heart. She felt her pulse speed up when her mother answered the phone.

"Hi, Mom," she said, trying to force herself to sound cheery when in reality her guts were in an uproar. She'd honestly thought she'd never speak to either of them again. "It's Erica."

"I thought we made it clear we had nothing to say to you."

"Wait, please don't hang up. Kyle's here."

"What do you mean he's there?"

"He said he ran away. I figured you'd probably be worried about him."

"I didn't even know he was gone. I thought he was upstairs in his room," her mother said, sounding anything but worried, and Erica's heart dropped. He'd told them. "But you know what? You can keep him for all I care. You two deserve each other."

Erica closed her eyes and continued holding the phone to her ear even though her mother had disconnected the call. She knew this was going to happen when he came out to them, but knowing it didn't stop the gut-wrenching pain she experienced. It had been one thing for them to turn their backs on her; she'd been twenty-eight when she told them. But Kyle was still a minor. She shuddered to think what might have happened to him if he'd stayed in Syracuse and ended up living on the streets.

"You didn't call them, did you?" he asked when he and Cass emerged from the bathroom. "I should have told you they wouldn't care. I heard them talking about sending me to some gay conversion camp their church supports."

"I'm glad you came here, Kyle," Erica said, taking a seat next to him on the couch. She put her arm around him and hugged him. She saw Cass watching them and looking a little uncomfortable with the situation so she forced a smile. She pulled back and looked him in the eye. "You know you can always come to me, right?"

"Yeah, that's why I'm here," he said with a nod. She saw the tears welling up, so in an attempt to not embarrass him, she stood and went to Cass.

"I should go. His ribs are bruised, but I don't think anything's broken." Cass watched him for a moment then looked at Erica, the discomfort in her eyes now replaced with what looked like genuine concern. "Are you guys going to be all right?"

"We'll be fine as soon as we can figure things out," Erica answered with a quick glance over her shoulder. "As I'm sure you've surmised, our parents aren't the unconditional love type of people. They were when I was growing up, but things change, I guess. People change."

Cass handed her a business card.

"Call me if you need anything. I spent less than an hour with him, but I got the impression he's a good kid. If I can help, I'd like to."

"Thank you." Erica felt like she might cry now. "I thought you didn't like kids."

"I don't like young kids," Cass said with a smile. "Give me a room full of unruly teenagers any day."

"I'm going to bed," Kyle said as he stood from the couch. "If it's okay with you."

"I'll talk to you later," Cass said to Erica.

"No, don't go. Just let me get him settled and we can talk, all right?"

Cass seemed reluctant, but she finally took the television remote Erica handed to her and made herself comfortable on the couch. After a moment, she put the remote on the coffee table without having turned on the TV.

"Thank you for what you did, Cass," Kyle said, his voice soft.

"You're welcome." Cass smiled at him, and Erica felt some of the gloom recede at the sight. "Just don't get into trouble again, because I might not be around next time."

"I'll see you again, right?"

Erica glanced at Cass who seemed to be having trouble coming up with a response. She let her struggle for a bit before taking mercy on her.

"Of course you will," she said. "Cass is a friend."

CHAPTER SIX

Cass sat on the couch for a few minutes, but then she got to her feet. She really should just go home. Family stuff wasn't her thing. Especially when it was someone else's family. She hadn't been blessed with a father of the year candidate by any means, but at least she was fairly sure he would have cared if she'd run away.

"Or not," she said under her breath. Who knew how he might have reacted? Other than the occasional kiss on the cheek when her mother was getting her ready for bed, he'd never shown any affection toward her. In fact, he'd made sure to tell her how worthless she was whenever he had the opportunity. The adult Cass knew it had been his way of trying to control her, just as he did everyone else, especially women. That didn't lessen the pain and emotional scars that developed when she was little though, and were still a source of pain now. She wondered now if he would have even noticed had she run away from home.

"Thank you for waiting," Erica said as she came through the living room and went straight to the kitchen. "Can I get you something to drink? I have water, Coke, milk, beer. I could make coffee if you'd like some."

"Water's fine," Cass said. A beer would hit the spot right about now, but she thought she should keep her wits about her if she was going to be alone with Erica. The attraction was definitely still there, but getting involved with someone who had familial obligations like this wasn't something she was interested in.

She took the glass from Erica before Erica took a seat at the other end of the couch. Cass watched her for a moment until Erica caught her looking.

"I think you're his new hero."

"Yeah, right."

"I'm serious. He didn't stop talking about you while I was making up the bed for him. The way he tells it, you're a superhero."

Cass smiled as the comment sunk in. It felt nice. She didn't know why, but she liked Kyle. It was almost as though they shared some kind of connection.

"Anybody would have done the same thing," Cass said, but she didn't really believe the statement. Society for the most part had evolved into a self-centered state. If it didn't affect you, then why get involved? She knew everyone wasn't so callous, but in her experience, the vast majority of people were.

"No. Not true, and you know it," Erica said. "And a lot of people around here would have turned their backs on him simply because he's gay."

"I'll admit it's probably easier to be gay in a big city, but I'd like to believe there are some good people left, even out here in the sticks."

"Obviously, there are, because you helped him."

Cass felt her cheeks flush. What the hell? She'd never reacted this way to a compliment before. She made the quick decision to just go with it.

"Thank you for that," Erica said. "Helping him, I mean."

"Where are you from, if you don't mind my asking?" Cass felt a change of subject was called for, because if things kept going in that vein, she may not be able to ignore the urge to kiss Erica for much longer.

"Syracuse, born and raised."

"How did Kyle get to Elba, which is where I rescued him, by the way."

"He borrowed money from a friend and bought a bus ticket to Batavia. His reasoning was that looking at a map, it was closer than either Rochester or Buffalo."

"Smart kid."

"Yes, he is."

"Are you going to send him back home?"

Erica was silent for a few moments, and Cass watched the emotions take over her features. She really was beautiful when she was concentrating on something. Hell, she was beautiful no matter what she was doing. When she let her head fall back against the couch, exposing her neck, it took everything in Cass to resist running her fingers along the skin.

"I don't think I can. My mother told me to keep him here, for all she cared. They don't want him, and hearing her say that breaks my heart."

"I'm sorry, but what a bitch. It should be a crime to treat your kids like that."

Erica laughed, and the sound sent a shiver through Cass's body. She wanted to hear the wonderful sound forever.

"She is a bitch, so don't be sorry for saying it out loud. My fantasy is to someday tell her exactly that to her face."

"Those aren't the kinds of things I fantasize about." The words were out of her mouth before she had the opportunity to stop them. Her cheeks flushed again.

"Are you flirting with me?" Erica smiled, and Cass noticed the dimples she hadn't seen before. They were adorable and only added to the overall sexiness Erica possessed.

"I'm not sure how to answer," Cass said honestly. She didn't want to scare her away, but then again, why not? *Because I like her, that's why not.* The thought should have had Cass running for the proverbial hills, but instead, a sense of calm washed over her. "I really need to get home."

"Oh, okay."

Cass thought she sounded disappointed. They both stood, and Erica walked her to the door, which was only a few feet away from where they'd been sitting. Before she opened the door, Cass turned to face her and found herself to be only a couple of inches from Erica. She glanced down to Erica's lips before sucking in a breath and meeting her eyes. She was almost certain she saw desire in those blue depths.

"I really want to kiss you right now," she said, and Erica's eyes darkened at the words. "Would that be okay?"

"I think it might be a bad idea." Erica looked as though she were struggling with the words, but Cass nodded and took a step back. "But if the invitation is still open, I'd love to have dinner with you sometime."

"Absolutely. How's Friday?"

"Perfect."

"Then it's a date. I'll pick you up at six."

Cass was almost to her car when the words she said finally hit home.

A *date*? She didn't date. And she'd be sure to set the record straight on Friday night. But there was a part of her that was feeling giddy about it. Really? Giddy? Cass shook her head.

"God help me."

Chapter Seven

I can't go with you tomorrow," Danny said, referring to the storage auction in Batavia they'd planned on attending. There were only a handful of units available, but they'd both been looking forward to it. Danny, especially, since he hadn't been able to go yet this year.

"Why? What's up?" Cass asked before taking a bite of the toast he'd made for her.

"Barb's mother is coming to see the baby." The look on his face told her all she needed to know about how he felt about his mother-in-law visiting. Since she lived in Virginia, it was pretty obvious it wasn't going to be a quick trip either. "She'll be here tonight."

"All the more reason for you to get out of the house."

"I wish," he said with a sad smile and a shake of his head. "Barb wants me here. You know they don't really get along well, and she wants me to run interference if things get too crazy."

"How long is she planning on being here?"

"A week."

Cass nodded, but she knew what he wasn't telling her. If she bought a unit in Batavia, she wouldn't be able to count on him to help clean it out. Her mind raced, trying to think of who she might be able to talk into going with her. She was coming up blank.

"Maybe I won't go either," she finally said.

"Why not?"

"If I buy a unit, who's going to help me with it? If there's anything big I won't be able to move it by myself."

"What about the kid you told me about? Lyle?"

"His name is Kyle, and I don't know if it would be such a good idea."

"You're having dinner with Erica tonight, right?" he asked. She nodded so he continued. "Talk to her about it. He's only been here a few days, so I doubt he'd have other plans. Just talk to her. What could it hurt?"

Cass thought about it. The only reason she was hesitating was because she figured if she involved Kyle in her work, she'd end up spending more time with Erica, and she wasn't sure that was a good idea. There was definitely a mutual attraction there, which was perfectly fine for a bit of fun, but what if Erica wanted more? Cass couldn't give her more.

"I'll talk to her," she said after a moment, but Danny gave her one of his looks. "What?"

"You like her. I can tell because you talk about her. You've never done that before."

"Yes, I have."

"No, you haven't. I assume you're not celibate, but you've never once talked about a woman before. I think you might finally be maturing."

"Fuck you," she said, barely resisting the impulse to throw the last bite of her toast at him. "I told you before I don't want a relationship. I like having the freedom to do as I please and not answer to anyone."

"It's not so bad, you know, having someone to come home to at night." He talked while he washed the few dishes they'd used for their breakfast. He looked over his shoulder at her. "Maybe you should give it a try. I just want you to be happy, Cass."

"I am happy," she said, knowing she sounded anything but. She stood and took her coffee cup to him.

"Bullshit," he replied. "I know why you avoid relationships, you know."

"Then enlighten me, little bro."

He shut the water off and dried his hands on the towel he always had flipped over his shoulder whenever he was doing dishes. She watched him in silence as he was obviously working out in his head how to put into words what he wanted to say without pissing her off. She knew this look. It was his trying to be diplomatic look. She was about to leave when he met her eyes and leaned back against the counter.

"You're worried you'll end up in a relationship like Mom and Dad's. I know she was never truly happy, and she felt trapped in her marriage. But you need to understand, times were different back then."

"Really, Danny? It was the eighties, not the fifties," she said. "It's not like women were still expected to be barefoot and pregnant all the time."

Cass saw what he was trying to do. He'd known she'd react to his statement the way she did. He was going to try to force her to look at the situation in a different way. It wasn't as though she'd never done it on her own, but it always ended up the same. It was because of their overbearing and abusive father that her mother had never been happy. There was nothing he could say to change history.

"You're right," he said with a quick nod. "Which only means she was somewhat to blame for staying with him, don't you think?"

"He didn't give her a choice, Danny. Did you know she was going to leave him once? I was thirteen at the time, and you were eleven," she said, silently cursing him for making her remember the day she'd tried for years to forget. "She'd packed a bag for the three of us. She was getting ready to walk out the door when he came home early. It was the only time I ever saw him hit her, but I'm sure there were other incidents."

"Her black eye?" Danny asked. It was apparent he hadn't known what really happened that day. Their mother explained the black eye on a clumsy accident, and she knew Danny believed it. Cass knew differently, but she was forced to act like she believed her mother's explanation.

"Yeah. He told her she'd regret it if she left him. He'd make sure she'd never see her kids again." Cass wiped her eyes of the tears she'd shed because of the memory.

"He said it while you were there with her?"

"He didn't know I was there. When she saw him pull into the driveway, she sent me to the kitchen. I was listening just inside the doorway. He threatened to kill her, Danny. He said he would hunt her down like a dog and make sure she never took another breath."

"I didn't know," he said, his voice quiet. Cass noticed his eyes filling with tears as well.

"I know you didn't. So don't assume you know anything about my private life. I will not get trapped in a relationship with someone who wants me to conform to the person they want me to be."

"But have you ever even let anyone close enough to find that out about them?" Danny crossed his arms over his chest as he spoke. "Not everyone is a control freak like he was."

"I did once."

"And what happened?"

"She tried to force me to be someone I wasn't. She claimed she wanted to be with me, but she didn't want her friends or family to know she was gay. She wanted me to look and act like I was heterosexual, and to tell everyone we were friends."

"And what happened?" he asked again, beginning to sound like a broken record.

"I left her." Cass knew where he was headed with this line of questioning, so when he started to speak again, she shook her head and held her hands up to stop him. "I don't want to hear it, Danny. Just keep your opinions to yourself."

Cass turned and walked out the back door without another word and headed back to her cabin. She knew he would point out that because she'd been the one to leave, it proved she would never allow herself to get into a bad relationship. Cass already knew that, damn it, but what Danny didn't know about was the way their father treated her whenever no one else was around. To him, she was nothing more than a servant. She was there for no other reason than to fetch his newspaper and bring him his slippers and his supper every night. Hell, she may as well have been a dog.

Her father had seen to it that she had no self-esteem growing up. She'd worked hard over the years to regain it, but there was always his voice in the back of her head reminding her no one could ever possibly love her. She was worthless. And there was a part of her that still believed those words, no matter how hard she tried to convince herself they weren't true. Those words were the reason she kept an emotional distance from the women she slept with. And they were why she rarely saw the same woman more than once.

But she was happy, damn it. When she walked into the cabin and Gordy jumped up and down, his tail wagging furiously in his excitement to see her, she dropped to her knees and ran her hands through his fur while he licked her face.

"We've got each other, right, buddy? That's all we need."

She found herself wishing her mother was there. She'd called her the day before to let her know Danny had brought Barb and the baby home from the hospital. Cass told her she didn't need to come home. The baby was fine. Barb was fine. Danny was fine. The only one who wasn't fine was Cass, but she'd never admit that to her mother. Her out of character attraction to Erica coupled with the fear Danny would stop doing storage auctions left Cass feeling as if her world was turned upside down. She had the feeling the only person who could help right it again was her mother.

"So you're going on a date with Cass?" Kyle asked with a grin as he watched her searching through her closet to find something to wear. He was sitting on her bed, Willie by his side enjoying the belly rubs Kyle was offering. Erica felt a little jealous the cat had taken to Kyle so quickly, which was ridiculous.

"I am," she answered, distracted. She had no idea where they were going, and therefore had no clue how she should dress.

"I like her."

"So do I." Erica smiled. She'd thought often of the night Cass told her she wanted to kiss her. She wondered where things might have gone if she'd let her. After giving herself a mental shake, she went back to pushing clothes around in the closet.

"She's hot."

"Excuse me?" Erica turned to see a big grin on his face. "I thought you were gay?"

"I am," he said with a shrug. "Doesn't mean I can't find a girl attractive. It also doesn't mean I want to sleep with her if I do."

"Kyle!" Erica said, but she found it hard to reprimand him.

He'd been living with her for the better part of a week, and he seemed happy. Certainly happier than she'd ever seen him since he'd come out to her. He was relaxed too, and she knew it was because she'd given him a safe haven. Erica had tried calling their parents again, more than once, but she was sure they'd blocked her number after her call the night Cass had shown up on her doorstep with him. And they hadn't returned any of her calls.

She wasn't sure what to do about the whole situation, but she had to do something. He'd need to get enrolled in school, but the schools had been closed all week because of the snow and sub-zero temperatures. She figured she'd have to get a lawyer too, to help her gain guardianship of Kyle. At this point, even if their parents did want him back, she wasn't sure she'd let him go after the way they'd treated him.

"What? I'm only stating a fact."

"You're fifteen. You shouldn't be having sex with anyone."

"I'm almost sixteen, and I haven't had sex," he said, looking appropriately embarrassed. "I just know I don't want to with a girl."

Erica shook her head because at his age, she'd known she *did* want to sleep with a girl. Her best friend since kindergarten, as a matter of fact. But the moment she'd told Debra Jenkins she was a lesbian, she'd stopped being her best friend. But at least Deb had kept her secret. Erica always figured it was because she didn't want to be accused of being a lesbian herself. Guilt by association.

"But Cass is hot. I mean, you think so too, right?" he asked after a moment.

"Yes," she answered, her mind flashing back to the other night again. Why hadn't she let Cass kiss her? She vowed to just go with it tonight, if Cass wanted to try again. "All right, get out of here. I need to shower and get dressed or I won't be ready when she gets here."

"If you really want to get her attention, wear the black dress with the plunging neckline," he said as he closed the door behind him.

What did he know of plunging necklines, a fifteen-year-old gay male? Still, she took it from the closet and held it up in front of her to see it in the full-length mirror.

Maybe he was right. It did look good. And it was certain to gain her a lot of attention.

CHAPTER EIGHT

Cass sat in her car for a moment, willing her palms to stop sweating. This was so not like her, to be nervous at the prospect of spending an evening with a beautiful, sexy woman. Of course, she hadn't been on many dates in her life. Dating wasn't an issue when you went to a bar, saw what you liked, and went home with her. An actual date wasn't a prerequisite for a one-night stand.

She tried not to think about the fact she was drawn to Erica in a way she'd never experienced before, because it was just nuts. She hardly knew her, but she was fully cognizant of the reality of the situation. Erica wasn't a one-night stand. Cass had the feeling Erica could never be a one-night stand, for her or anyone else. The realization should have sent her running back home, and she met her eyes in the rearview mirror as she waited for the panic to set in.

It never did.

She finally opened the door and got out, trying to smooth her slacks as she made her way to Erica's front door. She knocked quickly and took a step back, wondering if this was a mistake. Too late now, because she could hear the deadbolt sliding open.

"Come on in," Kyle said with a grin. "She isn't quite ready yet."

"It's okay. I'm a little early," Cass said. She took a seat on the couch and wiped her hands on her pants.

"Nervous?" he asked.

"No, why would I be nervous?"

He laughed and pushed his hair out of his eyes.

"Don't worry. She is too. You should've brought flowers or candy or something, don't you think?"

Damn it, why hadn't she thought of that? She glanced at the clock hanging on the wall and wondered if she had time to run to the store.

"I thought I heard someone at the door," Erica said as she entered the room. "You're early."

"I'm sorry…" Cass began, but her mouth went dry when she saw Erica. The black dress she was wearing hugged her in just the right way. And the neckline, well, it didn't leave much to the imagination, which was fine with her. She stood and took a step toward her. "You look absolutely stunning."

"Thank you," Erica said, her cheeks reddening slightly. "I just grabbed the first thing I saw in my closet."

They both started when Kyle stifled a laugh. Cass had completely forgotten he was there.

"I'm going to my room," he said. Just before he got there, he turned and looked at them again. "Have fun, but not too much fun. And don't do anything I wouldn't do. I won't wait up for you."

He closed the door and Cass turned her attention back to Erica. Her eyes were drawn to the cleavage on display. The dress plunged just enough to reveal the swell of her breasts, and the sight made Cass's mouth water. How strange it could be so very dry one second, and then watering the next. She didn't even try to stop her eyes from roaming all over Erica, who was watching her look, and Cass didn't care in the slightest.

"I take it you like what you see?" Erica asked.

"Very much," Cass admitted with a nod. She closed the distance between them, but then paused at the memory of being stonewalled a few nights ago. She met Erica's gaze and took her hand. It was warm and soft, and Cass never wanted to let go. "I am going to kiss you now. Are you planning to stop me again?"

"No."

Cass put her hand against the small of Erica's back and pulled their bodies together, all the while staring into her eyes. Erica's hands went to Cass's shoulders, then slid around until her fingers were playing with the hair at the nape of her neck. Cass watched as Erica's eyes closed, and her lips parted slightly, her head tipped back a little.

"God, you are so damn sexy," she said, mesmerized by the pulse she could see at her throat. It appeared Erica's heart was beating just as quickly as her own. Good to know she wasn't the only one having this reaction to their bodies being pressed together. Erica opened her eyes, and Cass lost her breath at how dark the blue had become.

"I thought you were going to kiss me," she said, her voice barely more than a whisper.

Cass leaned in and touched Erica's lips with her own, gently at first, but then Erica deepened it by running the tip of her tongue across Cass's lips. She groaned as she opened her mouth, allowing Erica inside. Cass felt her desire ratchet up a notch, and she slid her hands up Erica's back, searching for a zipper. When she finally found it, she tugged gently, but then Erica took a step back, shaking her head.

"Kyle."

It was the only word Cass needed to hear. She'd forgotten all about the young man in the next room. She glanced over her shoulder, but his door was still closed. As she straightened her shirt she met Erica's gaze.

"I'm sorry."

"Don't be," Erica said, reaching out and running a finger along her jaw. "Don't ever be sorry."

Cass fought to gain control of her raging hormones. She wanted Erica, and she knew the feeling was mutual, but as long as Kyle was there, it was never going to happen. The disappointment at the realization cut deeper than Cass expected it to.

"We should probably go," she said.

"Yes, we should."

❖

"Can I see you again?" Cass asked when they arrived back at Erica's house a few hours later.

"You'll see me tomorrow, won't you?" Erica asked. She'd agreed to let Kyle go with Cass to the storage auction as long as she could tag along. She'd seen the shows on television, but she was curious as to how it all worked.

"Not the same thing. Besides, your brother will be with us."

"I could make coffee if you want to come inside," Erica said, not ready for the evening to end quite yet.

"I'm not sure that would be a good idea."

"Why not?"

"Because I can't promise to keep my hands to myself."

Erica looked up at the house and saw the light in Kyle's room was on. It was close to midnight, so apparently he had waited up for her.

"Yeah, I guess it probably wouldn't be a good idea. I'm sorry."

"You have nothing to be sorry for," Cass told her. She reached over and took Erica's hand. "I had a good time tonight. And as much as I don't want it to end, I think it should. But I would like to do it again."

"So would I." Erica turned her hand over and entwined their fingers. She leaned across the gearshift and kissed Cass quickly on the lips. When she grabbed the handle to open the door, Cass held tightly to her hand.

"No, that was not an acceptable good night kiss," Cass said.

Erica held her breath as Cass shifted in her seat and leaned closer, only stopping when their lips were mere inches apart. The kiss was sweet, almost like a promise of things to come. She felt the throbbing between her legs that first started before they'd left the house earlier, and hadn't seemed to completely go away all night. It was back with a vengeance now, and Erica knew she was going to have trouble falling asleep.

"You are such an incredible kisser," Erica murmured against her lips, not wanting to fully end it.

"So are you," Cass replied. "I think I could spend the rest of my life kissing you."

Their tongues slid against each other and she moaned. She wanted nothing more than to drag Cass inside the house and straight to her bedroom, but she remembered her vow to take things slowly. It wouldn't be easy, but it was for the best, especially now that Kyle was in the picture.

"So, can we do this again?" Cass asked when they were finally forced to come up for air.

"God, yes."

"I meant dinner." Cass chuckled and squeezed her hand.

"But if I'm lucky, it will lead to more of this," Erica said.

"I certainly hope so."

"We'll see you bright and early in the morning."

"Yes, you will."

Erica took a deep breath and forced herself to vacate the car. When she got to the door, she looked back and saw Cass was waiting until she got inside. She quickly unlocked the door with shaking hands. She waved and then went inside. She'd barely gotten her coat off when Kyle came walking out of his room.

"Why didn't you invite her in?"

"First of all, it's none of your business," she said. She took off her shoes and walked to the kitchen for a glass of water, Kyle following right behind her. "And second, I did invite her in. She had to leave because she's getting up early in the morning so she can go to a storage auction."

"Cool," he said. "I think that would be an awesome thing to do."

"Really?"

"Sure. Those guys on TV make it look easy."

"I'm sure it's not so easy in real life, Kyle. But we're going to find out because she's taking us with her tomorrow."

"Are you serious?" Kyle's eyes went wide, and Erica smiled. He looked more like the child he used to be than a boy becoming a man. His excitement was palpable.

"Yes, I am, and she'll be here a little after seven in the morning, so I suggest you get some sleep," she said. She was surprised when he grabbed her and kissed her on the cheek, but it was nice. On the other hand, it made her sad to realize her own mother had thrown it all away. She watched him as he almost ran back to his bedroom. "She's probably going to put you to work, so just be ready."

"I will," he said before he closed his door.

Erica wondered if she should try to call her parents one more time before retaining a lawyer to gain guardianship. But what would be the point? She'd already tried to call them three or four times and got no answer, no return phone calls. It was obvious they didn't want him back, and that fact made her furious.

When they'd rejected her, it had hurt more than she thought possible. How could a fifteen-year-old kid possibly be expected to deal with his own parents rejecting him simply because of who he was? She'd do everything she could to make the transition easy for him, but she had a feeling he was going to be devastated when the realization of the situation finally sunk in.

Chapter Nine

"Just make sure you don't raise your hand, or nod your head once the bidding starts," Cass told them both as they were waiting for the first unit to be opened. She thanked whatever higher power there might be for Rodney not making an appearance at this auction. She really didn't want to deal with him while Erica and Kyle were there with her. "Actually, once the bidding starts, maybe you just shouldn't move at all."

"You're a laugh-riot, Cassidy Holmes," Erica said.

Kyle had still been in the shower when Cass arrived to pick them up that morning, so they'd had a few minutes to themselves. Unfortunately, those minutes flew by as Erica kissed her almost senseless. She'd been about to pick her up and carry her to the bedroom when they heard the water shut off.

"I do my best." Cass flashed her a smile that was both sexy and innocent at the same time.

"Your best is pretty damn good," Erica said, leaning close to her so no one else could hear the seductive comment.

Cass felt her cheeks flush and she shifted her weight from one foot to the other trying to hide her embarrassment, because she was pretty damn sure Erica wasn't referring to her comedic skills. She was saved further humiliation when the auctioneer started his spiel about how no one could enter the unit, you'd only have a few seconds to look it over, blah, blah, blah. She'd heard it so many times she tuned him out. Erica and Kyle were seemingly enthralled by it though.

"Listen," she said as she pulled them both aside. "If you see anything interesting in these units, don't say anything. Wait until we walk away and tell me quietly what you saw, all right?"

They both nodded but seemed anxious to see what was in the unit. She let them go, shaking her head and trying not to laugh. She remembered her first time at one of these auctions. She'd been twelve, and her best friend's father bought storage units for a living. Damn, had it really been over twenty years ago? She'd been fascinated with everything about it, and started buying her own units at eighteen.

There was nothing of interest for her in the first couple of units, even though Kyle had gotten a little excited over the boxes in the very front of the second one. There was one for a forty-two-inch flat screen TV, a couple of boxes for laptops, and one for a PlayStation 4. He grabbed her arm and asked her why she wasn't bidding on it. She promised to explain it to him when the auction was over.

The third unit though, looked promising. There was furniture, high end stuff, no less. She knew she could sell it if she got the locker for a decent price. She saw a washer and dryer. The refrigerator would be a bitch to move, but she could easily get a hundred dollars for it. There were tools again, and who didn't want tools? And she was pretty sure she saw what looked like the front end of a snowmobile. It was hidden really well behind the furniture, so she couldn't be one hundred percent positive, but she was willing to gamble on it.

Kyle looked so excited she was finally bidding on something, she was sure he wasn't taking into consideration the amount of work it was going to take to clean it out. She just hoped Erica had told him he wasn't here only as an observer. He'd be joining in on the fun.

She thought about letting it go when the bidding reached five hundred, but the look on Kyle's face when she didn't bid right away almost broke her heart. She raised her hand to bid five fifty. The other guy dropped out then, and she took a relieved breath as she went to place her own padlock on the door.

"That was so freaking awesome," Kyle said.

"You might not think so when you're helping me load all this crap into the truck later," she told him. She flung her arm around his shoulders as they walked to the next unit.

"Yeah, I will," he answered, sounding sure of himself.

It ended up being the only unit she bought for the day, but it looked like it would be a good profit for her. The snowmobile was almost new, and there had been a large flat screen TV and a gaming console in there too. Even though she knew she could sell it, Kyle seemed so excited about the PlayStation 3, she'd decided to let him keep it. She wasn't going to let him know until they'd gotten back home though.

"So why didn't you bid on the unit with all the electronics boxes?" Kyle asked while they were loading up the truck.

Cass leaned against the wall of the unit and looked around, noticing they'd gotten everything but the big items. The easy part was over. Now came the backbreaking portion of the day.

"Chances are those boxes were empty," she told him. Erica took a seat on a newer looking sofa and Cass smiled at her.

"Why would someone put empty boxes in a storage unit?" Erica asked.

"Most states, New York included, mandate that all money these places get at auction over and above the cost of arrears due them, and their cost to contact the owner and place ads about the auction, has to go to the person who rented the unit in the first place."

"So you can rent a unit, not pay for it, and then if the storage facility gets more than what's owed, the person who stopped paying gets the excess?" Erica asked. Cass nodded and noticed they both looked a bit perplexed.

"People have started to wise up about the law, so they stage the unit before they stop paying," Cass explained. "They place empty boxes for desirable electronic items in the front of the unit, and then the bidding usually goes sky high."

"Like it did today," Kyle said. "But how do you know somebody didn't really store their electronics in those boxes?"

"You can't really know for sure," Cass admitted with a shrug. "You're taking a gamble either way. I'm going to share something I was told when I first started doing this. Most people will put the really valuable items in the back corners, usually on the right side of the unit. I've found it to be true more than seventy-five percent of the time."

"How did you learn the trick about the empty boxes?" Erica asked, and Cass chuckled.

"The hard way. Danny and I bought a couple units like that only to be sorely disappointed when we opened the boxes up. Trust me, you learn real quick when you realize you're throwing your money away."

"What's the most interesting thing you've ever found in a unit?" Kyle asked.

Cass glanced at Erica. She knew the look in his eye. He'd had his interest piqued, just as she had twenty years earlier. Erica didn't know it yet, but her little brother was destined to become an auction hunter.

"Most of the time we're lucky if we make a profit at all," she answered honestly. She wasn't about to give him false hope. "But then once in a while you find something to bring in a tidy sum. *Those* units are the ones we keep coming back for. We're always looking for the item that might bring us six figures."

"Have you ever found one?" Erica's eyes were wide with excitement.

"No, and I'm fairly certain we won't here in western New York. Not unless we came across a unit owned by one of the Bills or Sabres, anyway. But then why wouldn't they pay their storage bill every month?" Every unit they bought stoked the fire in her belly, even though she knew their chances of finding a real treasure was slim to none, and slim just walked out the door, as her father always said whenever she'd ask him for money. But it didn't stop her from dreaming. "And you've got to remember, people who have the money to buy those high priced electronics probably have the room to keep them in their houses. They wouldn't need to rent a storage unit for them."

Kyle only nodded as he stood and went out to the truck. He came back a moment later with the hand truck so they could move the appliances and heavy furniture. He wheeled it to the refrigerator and then turned to face her.

"You never told us what the most interesting thing you ever found was," he said.

"Most interesting, or most expensive?"

"Both."

"Well, we bought a unit owned by a little old lady who had died. Her entire art collection was packed in boxes. There weren't a lot of original pieces in it, but what there was brought us around fifty thousand dollars when all was said and done."

"Damn," Kyle said, then he looked at Erica with a sheepish expression. "Sorry, but the moment seemed to call for it."

Cass laughed but quickly stifled it when she received a rather stern look from Erica. She wondered briefly if Erica would be so serious in the bedroom.

What? Where the hell had that come from?

"As far as the most interesting, I would have to say the dead body we found in a casket last fall," Cass said, unable to stop the shudder running through her body. The nightmares finally stopped about a month afterward, but it still gave her the heebie-jeebies to think about it.

"I remember hearing something on the news about that," Erica said, looking horrified. "Oh, my God, it was you?"

"Yes, it was, I'm sorry to say. The coffin was with a bunch of Halloween decorations, so neither of us thought much about it, except whoever owned it must have been a little strange. I never expected to find a real body inside of it. In fact, Danny and I both thought it was a dummy until the stench reached us."

"Okay, enough," Erica said, her stern side coming out again. She stood and walked toward the door of the unit. "I think you've just fueled my nightmares for the next six months. I'm going to wait in the truck for you two to finish here."

"Did you touch it?" Kyle asked when Erica was out of earshot.

"What? No. Hell no," she said. She could only imagine what her face looked like by the way he laughed at her reaction. She smiled then. "But at least I didn't go running out of the unit screaming like my brother did. I thought for sure he was going to have a heart attack."

They both laughed then, and Cass thought to herself she could get used to having this kid around. She allowed the idea to bounce around her head for a moment. She knew the mere thought of it should scare the hell out of her, but it didn't.

And that realization *did* scare the hell out of her.

CHAPTER TEN

Erica insisted they go home with her so they could help unload everything. Cass warned them her brother's mother-in-law was visiting, so who knew if Danny would have time to help her do it anytime soon. Had she known Danny would insist on them staying for dinner, she never would have offered to help unload. She felt out of place because she didn't know these people, but they seemed nice enough.

When they were done eating, Barb went upstairs to rest. Danny and Cass stood side-by-side at the sink washing the dishes. Who didn't have a dishwasher in this day and age? She knew she'd probably let the dishes pile up until she ran out of clean ones if she didn't own one. She and Kyle sat at the kitchen table watching them.

"Thank you again for dinner, Danny. It was wonderful," she said.

"It was my pleasure, believe me," he said with a glance over his shoulder. "Cass has never brought home a girl she was dating before."

Kyle gave her leg a nudge with his foot, and when she looked at him, he was smiling and nodding. She rolled her eyes and refocused her attention on Cass and Danny. She had to admit, it was an interesting piece of news to hear, but she was in no way ready to let anyone know exactly how interesting she found it.

"Maybe because I've never dated anyone before," Cass said, giving Danny a punch to the upper arm.

"Ouch!" Danny rubbed the spot with his other hand and glared at her, but Cass was laughing at him. Erica saw what was coming before Cass did, but it happened too quickly for her to tell Cass to look out. Danny grabbed the dishtowel he had flung over his shoulder and in one swift move, snapped it against her leg.

"You asshole," Cass said, still laughing at him.

Just when Erica thought a war might break out, Barb's mother, Judy, came bursting through the door looking as though she wanted to string somebody up by their toes.

"Are you *trying* to wake the baby up?" she asked in a whisper-yell Erica had never experienced before. She found herself thankful she wasn't a member of this family. Judy stalked over to the sink and poked a finger into Danny's chest. "I had you wash the dishes to keep you busy, not to fool around and make enough noise to raise the dead."

"It was my fault, Judy," Cass said. She bowed her head slightly and had her hands clasped behind her back. She reminded Erica of a little girl getting a scolding.

"Maybe you should go home then," Judy said, sounding angrier by the moment. "Lord knows your brother doesn't need any help getting in trouble."

"Judy—" Danny began, but she cut him off before he could get anything else out.

"For the life of me, I don't know what Barb sees in you. You don't work, and as far as I can tell, you refuse to get a job. Give me one good reason why I shouldn't take her and the baby back to Virginia with me."

"He has a name," Danny said. Erica had to give him credit. She was sure his mother-in-law scared the crap out of him, but it was apparent he wasn't about to back down.

"Excuse me?" Judy took a step back, clearly not accustomed to anyone standing up to her. What a joy it must have been for Barb to grow up with Judy as a mother.

"I said, the baby has a name. I'd appreciate it if you'd use it."

"I don't like the name you chose."

"Really?" Danny squared his shoulders and took a step toward her. "I didn't pick the name. Barb did. So if she chose to name him after my great-grandfather, I can't help it."

"But I'm sure you did nothing to dissuade her from making such a horrid choice, did you?"

"Why should he have?" Erica asked, shocking herself by speaking up. Judy seemed even more surprised than she was at her joining the conversation uninvited, so Erica stood and went to stand next to Danny.

"I don't recall asking for an opinion from you or anyone else," Judy said with a pointed look at Kyle and then Erica. "Who are you again?"

"Her name is Erica, and she's Cass's girlfriend," Danny told her, obviously irritated with the fact Judy couldn't be bothered to remember someone's name for an hour.

"Girlfriend. Right." Judy managed to make those two words drag out as though they had a combined ten syllables. She gave a little shake of her head and met Danny's eyes again. "Just another reason for me to insist Barb comes home with me."

"You aren't taking Barb, or Clarence, anywhere," Danny said.

"I do wish you'd stop calling him that."

"It's his name," said Cass, finally stepping forward to stand on Danny's other side. Erica was beginning to wonder if she was going to defend her brother at all. "And it isn't going to change, no matter what you do."

Judy looked between the three of them as though they'd all lost their minds. Yep, Erica thought. She is definitely used to getting her own way. *Not this time, sweetie.*

"We'll see. And I don't want *these people* around my grandson."

"Excuse me?" Cass asked. Erica had the feeling she was fighting to keep her anger coiled up, but was close to losing the battle. "*These people?* He's my nephew, and in all honesty, I don't want *you* around him. How do you like that?"

Judy simply smiled at Cass as if she were mentally disabled and in need of pity. Erica wanted nothing more than to slap the woman, but she wouldn't. Not only was it not her place, but she would never stoop to Judy's brand of bullying.

"Oh, isn't this sweet. Daniel needs to have his sister step up for him." Judy turned her attention to Erica for a moment before dismissing her completely. "And her girlfriend, too."

"I want you out of my house," Danny said, the muscles in his jaw clenching rapidly.

"Fine," she said, turning for the door. She stopped but didn't look back. "I'll let Barb know to pack her things and we'll be gone first thing in the morning."

Danny started to go after her, but Cass grabbed his arm tightly and held him in place. He tried to pull free, but she tightened her grip.

"Let me go," he said. "I need to stop her."

"Do you really think Barb will let her get away with this?" Cass asked. She loosened her grip when she felt Danny relax a little. "Barb isn't going anywhere, and you know it. I've heard the way she talks about Judy. She would never allow her to take Clarence, or force her back to Virginia. Barb loves you, and you have a son you have to raise. Together. Don't do anything stupid you'll regret for the rest of your life, like saying something horrible to your wife about what a bitch her mother is."

The adrenaline obviously drained from him at that point, because she had to hold on to him when his knees buckled. Erica grabbed his other arm and they led him over to the table, where Kyle pulled out a chair for him.

"Jesus, did I really just stand up to her?" he asked, looking a little green around the edges.

"We all did," Cass answered. "And I don't know about you, but I feel awesome about it."

"It was wicked cool," Kyle said quietly.

"It was, wasn't it?" Danny offered a small smile, but to Cass it looked like he wanted to throw up. She slapped him on the back and laughed.

"I thought so," she said. All three of them looked at Erica, waiting for her response. Cass felt some of her defenses drop when Erica grinned sheepishly.

"Wicked cool," she said with a nod.

Chapter Eleven

Cass was standing on Danny's deck, her forearms resting against the railing and cursing the cold but enjoying it at the same time. It helped to clear her head. Judy always knew how to get under her skin, and Cass seemed powerless to remain immune to her snarkiness. She glanced over her shoulder when she heard the sliding glass door open and smiled when she saw Erica walking toward her.

"Hey," she said, returning her attention to the yard and wishing she was at her cabin with Erica. Alone. "I'm sorry about all that with Judy."

"I take it she really dislikes her daughter's choice in husbands," Erica said as she joined her. Cass glanced at her and took note of the fact she was resting against the railing exactly like she was.

"You're being far too diplomatic," Cass said with a wry grin. She took a deep breath and watched the steam as she exhaled. The cold burned her lungs, but it felt good. It made her feel alive. Or maybe the effect was simply because Erica was at her side. "Judy hates my brother, and by extension, me. Or she may only hate me because I'm a lesbian. I never bothered to ask, so I'm not really sure."

"Well, I for one am happy you're a lesbian."

"Yeah?" Cass smiled. She turned toward Erica and rested her hip on the railing. "Can I tell you a secret? I'm happy about it too."

Cass glanced toward the house to make sure no one was watching them before she moved closer and placed her palm against Erica's cheek. She felt Erica place a hand on her chest just above her breasts. She half expected her to push her away, but then Erica grabbed on to her jacket and pulled her close. Their lips were mere centimeters apart, and she could feel Erica's breath against her lips.

"I so want to be alone with you right now."

"Why is that?" Cass asked, teasing.

"Because I want to play Monopoly with you."

Cass laughed out loud at the absurdity of the statement, and at the way Erica said it so seriously. God help her, she liked Erica. Probably more than was prudent given her own feelings on relationships.

"We could leave Kyle here and go to my place," Cass said, hoping the mood hadn't been completely ruined. Erica looked surprised.

"You don't live here?"

"Well, I live here," she answered, spreading her arms toward the backyard. She then pointed toward the house Danny and Barb lived in. "I just don't live here."

"So you're telling me you sleep in the backyard? In a tent or something?"

"No, smartass." Cass grinned at the look of disbelief Erica was sporting. "See the light out there? It's attached to the cabin I live in. It's a really awesome place, just one big open area with a loft where my bedroom and the master bath are located."

Cass watched Erica as she was apparently weighing her options. It was only nine o'clock on a Saturday night, and she was sure Danny wouldn't have a problem playing video games with Kyle for an hour. Or maybe two. Erica finally met her eyes and shook her head with what Cass interpreted as disappointment.

"Honestly, I'd like nothing better than to go to your place and play Monopoly, but I don't think I should. Kyle would know what we were doing, and he'd tease me mercilessly."

"For playing Monopoly?" Cass shook her head. "I'll never understand kids today."

"Can I take a rain check?"

"Make it a snow check and you've got a deal." Cass used her thumb to brush a snowflake off Erica's cheek.

"I'm worried spring is never going to come."

"It will. It might not be until July, but it will arrive someday."

"If I kissed you right now, would it cause more problems for Danny with his mother-in-law?"

"It might, but I don't really care."

Cass stayed where she was as Erica stepped into her, pressing their bodies together. The heavy jackets they were wearing did nothing to diminish the excitement Cass felt. She was unusually warm, especially between her legs. The heat spread deliciously through her body when Erica's lips met hers.

No one had ever caused Cass to feel dizzy from a simple kiss. But Erica seemed to excel at doing just that. She was quickly becoming addicted to the way Erica kissed her. Without breaking the kiss, Cass unzipped both their jackets and slid her arms around Erica's waist, pressing even harder against her body. The frigid air was all but forgotten in the heat between them. When Erica ended the kiss, Cass groaned at the loss of her.

"I think I could kiss you forever," she said, resting her forehead against Erica's. Her breathing was erratic, and she didn't even try to hide it. "You are so freakishly awesome at it."

"Yeah? I had a real hard time choosing my major in college. I kept trying to decide between business or kissing. I guess I made the right choice?"

"Most definitely," Cass assured her with a sigh. "So you need a degree in kissing to play post office as an adult?"

"Hey, you guys, aren't you freezing your asses off?" Danny called from the door.

"Not really." Cass was reluctant to pull away from Erica, but if she didn't, she was afraid she might have to carry her to her cabin. She zipped her jacket up again and took Erica's hand to lead her back into the house. When she walked past Danny, she lowered her voice. "Your timing sucks, man."

"Barb tells me that all the time," he said with a nudge of his elbow.

"TMI, dude," she told him with a grimace. "I'm probably going to have nightmares now."

Danny just laughed as he followed them back into the house. He grabbed them each a beer from the fridge and took a soda out for Kyle.

"Is it okay if Kyle has this?" he asked Erica. She nodded and took the beer he held out to her. She didn't feel like she could talk without giving away how sexually aroused she was.

"What game are you guys playing, and where's the monster-in-law?" Cass asked. They walked into the living room where Kyle was playing the game on his own. They all sat before Danny answered, his voice quiet.

"She went to bed. Barb told her she needed to leave in the morning and made it clear she and Clarence would not be accompanying her." He looked at the stairs, and Cass knew he was worried she would come down. "Do me a favor and keep your voices down. I'm not in the mood to deal with her again tonight."

"I'm sorry I got involved in your family matters earlier," Erica said.

"Don't apologize, please," he said with a dismissive wave. "I wanted to thank you for standing up to her. Not many people have the guts to do it."

"I know I don't," Cass said.

"I was afraid I might be making things worse for you," Erica said.

"Not possible where Judy's concerned, trust me," Cass told her. "She's been trying to break them up since the day he and Barb met. She thinks we're all just white trash because we live out here in the sticks. She's made it quite clear had Barb not married Danny, she would never have been forced to socialize with such heathens. Danny and I are going to hell, did you know that?"

"Well, so am I, as I'm sure my mother and father would tell you," Erica said. "Well, of course, if they would stoop so low as to admit they had a daughter in the first place."

"Judy questioned why Mom wasn't here too," Danny said after a moment. Cass looked at him, knowing he'd no doubt been just as mad when Judy asked the question as she was now.

"Are you serious? Does she even admit she refused to come to your wedding? At least both of our parents were there for that. She has no right to criticize anyone," Cass said, barely able to control her resentment for Judy. It had damn near broke Barb's heart when her mother hadn't shown up for what should have been the happiest day of her life. Cass and her own mother were the ones who had comforted Barb then. "If I wasn't so scared of her, I'd go wake her up and give her a piece of my mind."

"It's the sentiment that counts, right?" Danny laughed quietly. "And those are my sentiments exactly. She scares the crap out of me, and I'm not afraid to admit it."

"You guys are too funny," Kyle said from his spot on the floor without tearing his eyes away from the television screen where his character was shooting monsters without missing a beat. "She didn't seem so scary to me. She's just a bitter old woman who wants a better life for her daughter than she had. I'm not saying you can't give it to her, but that's what she thinks."

"Nice save, Kyle," Erica said to him.

"Move over, kid," Danny said. "I want back in this game."

"Hey, Danny." Cass smiled at Erica and gave her a wink. "You mind if Kyle stays here while I show Erica my cabin?"

"What if Kyle wants to see it too?" Kyle asked.

"Really?" Erica said. "You're referring to yourself in third person now?"

"I'll give you a tour next time," Cass told him as she stood and held a hand out to Erica.

Danny nudged Kyle with an elbow and chuckled. "I think they want to be alone, if you understand what I'm saying."

"Okay, too much information," Kyle said and began chanting so he couldn't hear them.

"Come on," Cass said, leading her back to the kitchen so they could grab their coats and head out the back door. "Is this all right with you?"

"It's more than all right," Erica assured her, her voice huskier than normal.

Cass felt her knees actually weaken at the predatory look Erica favored her with. No one had ever caused that reaction in her. Never.

Cass tried to ignore the niggling thought that she might very well be traveling down a road she couldn't come back on. Erica didn't know it, but she had the power to completely wreck Cass, and Cass worried she might do just that.

Chapter Twelve

Erica followed Cass down a path too narrow for them to walk on side by side. She'd be so happy when all this snow melted. Syracuse always got its fair share of snow, but being here, about an hour away from Buffalo and Lake Erie, and even closer to Lake Ontario, the results of lake effect snow could be paralyzing. From listening to other people talk around town, this was the worst winter they'd had in years. Record temperatures, on the low side, not the high, snow that seemed to go on forever, and the wind? It was fairly calm tonight, but just the thought of how it had been blowing most of the time since she'd arrived here caused a shudder to run through her body.

Erica was watching her feet, worried she might slip on some ice and not wanting to make a fool of herself, so when Cass came to a sudden stop in front of her, she had no way of avoiding the crash that followed. At least they were both able to stay on their feet.

"Sorry," she mumbled through the scarf she had covering the lower part of her face. "Why did you stop?"

"I guess I probably should have asked you this before, but you aren't afraid of dogs, are you? Or allergic?" Cass said after turning to face her.

"The answer is no on both counts. Why?" Erica asked, a little concerned by the look of apprehension on Cass's face. "Is your dog vicious? Will he, or she, try to rip my throat out?"

"No," Cass laughed. It was a wonderful sound, and Erica hoped she'd get to hear it more often. "Gordy's a lover. The only two things you have to worry about are the fact he thinks he's a lap dog, and there's a real possibility he may just lick you to death."

"What kind of dog is he?" Erica asked, feeling some of that apprehension herself now. She pictured a huge Rottweiler, or maybe a Great Dane greeting them at the door. *Oh, Christ. What if it's a Saint Bernard?* She didn't necessarily have anything against any of those breeds, but if one knocked her down in order to lick her face, they could do a lot of damage.

"Golden retriever. Come on. I know he hears us, and if I don't unlock the door in the next thirty seconds, he's going to start barking his fool head off." Cass pulled the keys out of her pocket and went the remaining distance to the front door of her cabin.

It looked quaint on the outside, yet Erica had a feeling the inside would be much bigger than it appeared. She didn't get the impression Cass would be happy in a cramped space. Especially with a big dog being underfoot all the time.

As soon as Cass opened the door, a flash of gold came flying out and ran right past them. They both watched as the dog ran around in circles trying to find a suitable place to relieve himself.

"Gordy, where are your manners?" Cass called out to him. At the sound of her voice, the dog stopped abruptly and looked over, almost as if seeing them for the first time. "We have company, man."

Gordy tilted his head and studied Erica then. She made sure not to look him in the eye, because she'd heard dogs would take it as a challenge and feel the need to assert their dominance over you. After a moment, he took a couple of tentative steps toward Erica.

"Hold your hand out to him," Cass told her. "Let him smell you, but don't try to pet him until he decides you're okay."

"I've never had a dog," she whispered, casting an apprehensive look in Cass's direction.

"There's nothing to worry about, I promise," Cass said close to Erica's ear. The whisper of breath across her cheek threatened to be Erica's undoing. "He's not going to hurt you; he just needs to check you out before he allows you to touch him."

Erica wasn't afraid of dogs; she simply hadn't been around very many of them in her life. She'd never been allowed to have a pet other than a goldfish, and be real, what kind of a pet was a goldfish? Kittens and puppies you could snuggle with. What could you do with a goldfish other than watch it swim in circles day after day? Willie seemed to be enough pet for her now, but she'd never allowed herself to get too friendly with dogs. Willie and his attitude wouldn't like it if she came home smelling of canine.

"I have a cat," she said suddenly. "He isn't going to freak out about it, is he?"

"No, he likes cats."

"As friends, or as dinner?" Erica watched as Gordy sniffed her outstretched palm and pushed her hand around with his nose. After a moment, he stepped back and looked up at her, tail wagging somewhat hesitantly. He stretched forward and rested his chin in her hand, his brown eyes still looking up at her. Her heart melted. "Aren't you just the sweetest puppy?"

"Before you two fall in love, would you care to see the inside of my humble home?"

Gordy took off around the corner of the cabin, presumably to find the perfect pee spot, and Erica followed Cass inside. Cass waited at the door until Gordy returned, then shut it tight against the cold. Erica watched her as she removed her coat before holding a hand out for hers. Erica quickly shrugged out of it and passed it over for her to hang up.

Gordy took off toward his food bowl, and Erica let her eyes wander around the space. It was beautiful. It really was one big room, the only separation coming from a breakfast bar in the kitchen, and the sofa perfectly positioned about ten feet from the big-screen television mounted to the wall. She saw a staircase in the corner that presumably led to the bedroom, and she allowed herself a moment to wonder if they'd end up there later.

"I'd offer a tour, but there really isn't much to it other than what you can see from right here." Cass walked to the couch and sat, patting the cushion next to her, encouraging Erica to join her. "Unless you'd like to see where I sleep."

"I'd love to, but not tonight." Erica couldn't believe the words had come out of her mouth. Maybe she really was turning over a new leaf and wanting to move slowly. Something told her Cass would be worth the wait. Physically *and* emotionally. She took a seat and wasted no time snuggling into Cass's side, her head resting against her chest.

"Are you sure?"

Cass ran a hand slowly up Erica's side, causing a sensory overload. Erica's vision went fuzzy around the edges, and her pulse quickened to the point where it was actually painful between her legs. She forced herself to sit up and backed away to the other end of the couch.

"Not if you keep touching me like that. I won't be sure of anything."

"Sounds like a plan to me." Cass grinned as she reached for her, but Erica shook her head.

"Can we just talk?" she asked.

"We're finally alone, and you want to talk?" Cass's tone was teasing, but Erica couldn't miss the disappointment in her eyes or her posture.

"I feel like we don't really know each other."

"What do you want to know? My favorite color? My favorite book?"

"I want to know what you're looking for in a relationship."

Cass went quiet then, and Erica worried she'd said something wrong. But how could she have? They were dating, right? She thought it a reasonable request.

"I don't want a relationship," Cass said as she looked away and pushed a hand through her hair. Erica felt her stomach drop. So she only wanted to get her in bed and then move on to someone else? Oh, hell no. "But you make me feel things I've never felt before. With you, I almost think a relationship could work."

"You almost think it could?"

"The only reference I have is my parents, yeah?" Cass stood and started to pace. Erica watched in silence, sensing she should let her say what she had to say and not interrupt. "They weren't happy. Not at all. But they never got a divorce, either. They stuck it out for me and Danny, and I watched my mother go into a tailspin of depression. I also watched my father get angrier and more disrespectful every day. He was not a nice man, Erica. He controlled my mother from day one. And when she got pregnant, she married him, because she didn't have any other choice. Her parents threw her out when she told them, and she had nowhere else to go.

"She gave up her dreams because of him, in order to raise his children in his house," Cass stopped pacing and met Erica's eyes. "She wanted to travel the world. Wanted to be a world famous artist someday. But he stifled her creativity. Whenever he'd see she was painting, he'd ruin the canvas. He was determined she'd be nothing more than the mother of his children. I will not end up in a relationship where the other person tries to take away my dreams."

"You're wrong, you know," Erica said.

"What do you mean?"

"Your parents aren't the only example you have to go by. What about Danny and Barb? It seemed pretty obvious to me they love and support each other."

"It's easier not to risk my heart than to find out I'd made a mistake."

"So what you're really saying is you don't want to get hurt," Erica said. When Cass gave no answer, Erica threw her hands up in the air. "Who does? I mean, seriously, Cass, who does?"

"What do you want out of a relationship?" Cass asked her. The sudden change, if not in subject but in turning the tables, startled Erica, but she refused to let on.

"I want what my parents had," she said without hesitation, but then corrected herself. "What they still have. But I would never turn my back on my children. They love each other very much. I have no doubt they would do anything for the other. Just not for me and Kyle."

"You want children?" Cass asked, sounding nervous.

"I don't know. If I were to find the right woman, and we both wanted it, then yes, I would love to have children." Erica was beginning to realize Cass was not that woman, no matter how much she wished she were. She obviously had phobias regarding commitment, and Erica wasn't sure she had the patience to try to change her mind. "Do you want children?"

"You're kidding, right?" Cass fell onto the couch and rested her head against the back of it, staring up at the ceiling. "Do you remember the night we met?"

Of course she did. Cass had admitted she was scared of small children. Erica had been hoping she was joking considering the way she was with Kyle.

"How do you know it wouldn't be different if the child was actually yours?" she asked, her voice quiet. After a moment, Cass sighed and turned her head to meet her eyes.

"I *don't* know," Cass admitted. "I never let myself think too much about having children of my own. While I know there are plenty of single mothers out there, I honestly don't think I could do it on my own. And then there's the whole relationship thing."

They stared at each other for a few moments, and to Erica, it felt as if all the air in the room became heavy. She wanted Cass, and she could tell Cass wanted her too. Even if it hadn't been obvious before, it was now in the way Cass ran her eyes along the length of Erica's body. But what would be the point in sleeping with her if it wasn't going to lead anywhere? What if they had sex, and then Cass moved on to her next conquest? Erica didn't think she could deal with that. She opened her mouth to say so, but the words she actually spoke surprised her.

"Look, I'm not saying the way you feel is wrong," she said. "Relationships can be scary. They definitely take a lot of work. You don't want a relationship, and I do, but I know this thing between us, whatever it is, isn't going to go away. Maybe we should sleep with each other and just see where it goes?"

Cass was looking at her as though she'd sprouted another head while she was talking. Strangely, Erica felt like maybe she had. Her suggestion was so completely out of character for her, but how could Cass possibly know?

"And what if where it went was nowhere? Friends with benefits, maybe?"

Cass looked odd, almost as if she didn't want it for the two of them either, but Erica refused to go there. Fantasizing about something that would probably never happen was dangerous. It was a fantastic way to ensure a broken heart. Erica couldn't speak. She knew answering in the affirmative was something Cass would see through, because she'd never been a good liar.

Cass scooted closer to her on the couch and turned so she was facing Erica. Erica didn't resist when Cass took her hand and brought it to her lips for a lingering kiss, their eyes boring into each other.

"You wouldn't be happy with that arrangement, am I right?" Cass smiled, but Erica didn't answer. Cass had never felt this strange ache in her heart before. Yes, she was holding fast to her no relationships mantra, but when she was sitting there next to Erica, she had to fight to keep herself from offering forever. This was foreign territory for her, and she was worried she'd say the wrong thing. "I can't give you what you want, no, what you *need*, but I know I'm not strong enough to say no if you want to pursue something physical with me. You are the sexiest, most beautiful, most alluring woman I've ever met."

"I bet you say the same thing to all the girls," Erica said. She smiled, but it didn't reach her eyes, and Cass shook her head.

"I don't. In fact, I've never said it to anyone before." She willed Erica to believe her. There was nothing she could say that would convince her she was telling the truth, so what else could she do? "We should probably get back up to the house."

Cass made a move to stand, but Erica gripped her forearm and held her in place. When Cass looked back at her, Erica was shaking her head.

"You're right. I don't think I would be happy with that arrangement, but I'd like to try," she said, moving her hand up Cass's arm as she spoke. When it reached her cheek, Cass leaned into the touch and closed her eyes. "I want you, Cassidy. If all you can give me is one night, then so be it."

"You deserve so much more," Cass said. What the hell? Why did she feel like she was going to cry? She cleared her throat and backed away from Erica's hand. "I wish I could give it to you. I want to, but I don't think I can. I'm afraid I'd only let you down, and I don't think I could live with myself if that happened."

Erica let go of her and dropped her head. Cass felt like someone had squeezed her heart and wouldn't let go. What was happening to her? Any other time, with any other woman, she would have carried her upstairs and undressed her. But even though she didn't know Erica very well, Cass could tell she was different.

"I'm sorry I'm not good enough for you," Erica said.

She stood and tried to brush past her, but Cass stopped her. She waited until Erica met her eyes, then she pulled her in for a hug.

"Jesus, Erica, if anything, I'm the one who's not good enough for you," she said into her ear before kissing her gently there. She felt Erica's arms go around her, pulling her tightly against her body. This hadn't been what she was hoping for when she hugged her, but her body responded. Her pulse sped up, and she moved her mouth to Erica's neck. Erica groaned and pulled away enough to frame Cass's face with her hands. Her eyes were half closed with desire, and then she was kissing her.

Cass was powerless to stop it, even if she'd wanted to. Erica moved her hands down her body until she was tugging at the bottom of Cass's sweatshirt. Without thinking about what she was doing, Cass lifted her arms so Erica could remove it. Then they crashed together again, tongues fighting for dominance. Cass tensed slightly when she felt Erica's fingers brush across her bare flesh just before she started working on unbuttoning her jeans.

Cass took a step back and took over the job herself, sensing Erica's frustration. In a matter of a few seconds, Cass stood before her, naked. Exposed. Vulnerable. She resisted the urge to cover herself when Erica dropped her gaze, first to her breasts, then to the apex of her thighs.

"I need you," Erica said, her voice barely more than a whisper, causing Cass's pulse to spike. She slowly brought her eyes back up and licked her lips. "Please."

The one word nearly caused Cass to lose all control, especially coupled with the wanting she could so clearly see in Erica's eyes. She watched as Erica began unbuttoning her own shirt, but then her cell phone rang. Erica froze and Cass grabbed her pants, fumbling until she finally located the phone and answered it. She was going to kill him.

"Danny, this better be good."

"I just wanted to tell you not to rush back. I talked Kyle into staying the night, so you two just enjoy yourselves, and we'll see you up here for breakfast in the morning."

Danny disconnected the call then, and Cass looked at Erica.

"Is Kyle all right?" she asked, her concern obvious.

"He's fine." Cass wasn't sure if she should get dressed again or not. She felt a little foolish being the only one naked, but Erica hadn't given any indication the moment had truly passed. "Danny talked him into sleeping there so we could have some time alone."

Cass couldn't tell if Erica's furrowed brow was a good thing or not, but she sensed it didn't bode well for where the night had been going. She didn't have to wait long to find out.

"I should get him and go home." Erica buttoned her shirt back up again and walked toward the front door as Cass scrambled to put her clothes on.

"Erica, wait, I'll go with you."

"No, it might be better if you didn't."

"I picked you up this morning, remember?" Cass asked as she zipped up her jeans then pulled her sweatshirt over her head. She ran her hands through her hair and walked to the door, grabbing both their jackets and handing Erica hers. "Do you intend to walk home?"

"I'm sorry," Erica said.

"Don't be. It's been a long day." Cass shoved her hands in her pockets and forced a smile. "I don't blame you for forgetting."

"I meant about—"

"I know what you meant, and there's still no reason to apologize, okay?"

"Thank you," Erica said, looking relieved.

Cass sighed as they walked out the door, knowing this was going to be a long and sleepless night.

Chapter Thirteen

Cass stretched out on the couch when she returned home after dropping Erica and Kyle off. Kyle spent most of the fifteen-minute ride trying to get them to talk, but she and Erica both kept silent. Cass had wanted to talk to her but knew it wasn't appropriate with Kyle in the backseat, especially chattering away like he was. At least Erica possessed the manners to say good night when she got out of the car. Cass wished she could say the same about herself.

"Seriously? You couldn't just say good night?" Cass spoke to the empty room, but Gordy whined in response as he came to sit on the floor next to the couch, his chin resting on her stomach. She couldn't help but smile when she looked into his chocolate colored eyes. "At least I always know where I stand with you, right, boy?"

Gordy's ears perked up and his tail began thumping on the floor. Cass patted her thigh, which was all the encouragement he needed to jump up and make himself comfortable on top of her legs. He put his chin on her belly again and he closed his eyes when she started scratching behind his ears.

It was close to midnight, but she decided to stay there with him for a while before going up to bed. She closed her own eyes and tried her damnedest not to think about Erica Jacobs and all the things she was never going to get to do to her.

The loud banging on her door hadn't awakened her, but Gordy going nuts barking in response to the knocking made her bolt upright. Cass looked around the room, surprised to see the sun beginning to peek in through the closed curtains next to the front door. She rubbed her eyes and forced herself to stand just in time for the person outside to start banging again.

"Give me a damn minute!" she hollered, expecting it to be Danny. Who else could it possibly be at the ass crack of dawn on a Sunday morning? She stretched her back as she walked to the door and flung it open, surprised to find her mother standing before her, a huge grin on her face.

"Mom?" Cass couldn't believe what she was seeing. When Cass called her the other day, her mother gave no indication she was planning on showing up out of the blue.

"Are you going to let me in?" Sara Holmes was fifty-three years old and still as attractive as she'd ever been. Maybe even more so, Cass thought, since her husband had died two years ago. It was good to see her. She'd left the day after the funeral to travel across Europe and Asia before finally settling in Okinawa. Cass and Danny hadn't seen her since, but they spoke over the phone nearly every week.

"I'm sorry," Cass said before moving aside and motioning her to come in. She took the suitcases from her as she walked by and set them on the floor behind the couch. The next thing she knew, she was being enveloped in a warm hug. She melted into it, not realizing until that moment just how much she missed her mother. "You look good, Mom."

Her mother pulled away and smiled at her. She placed her hands on each side of Cass's head and just looked at her for a moment.

"You do too. You've grown into such a beautiful young woman, Cassidy. But you really shouldn't sleep in your clothes. It can be a bitch to get the wrinkles out."

"Coffee?" Cass asked, choosing to ignore the fact she was so observant. She somehow resisted the urge to try to smooth her clothes. Her mother nodded and released her before looking around the cabin. Cass made her way into the kitchen to start the coffee maker. Some of their best conversations had been had over a hot cup of coffee in this very cabin. Cass had lived there since she'd graduated high school. It had been her mother's suggestion, one her father hadn't wanted to agree to, but he finally did because Cass offered to pay rent. Her mother would come visit most mornings and they'd have coffee together.

"I really like what you've done to the place," her mother called from the far side of the room, near the stairs leading up to the master bedroom. Cass glanced over her shoulder at her and saw she was admiring the bookshelves Cass had built into the space under the stairs. Her mother picked up a book and read the back of it. "Still reading romances, I see."

"Yeah," Cass answered. "Old habits and all."

Danny loved giving her a hard time about her choice of reading material. He couldn't seem to understand why someone so against falling in love could be so enamored reading books about romance. She'd long ago realized that even though she wasn't going to get a happy ever after, it didn't mean she had to give up hope for other people.

"So," her mother said as she sat at the kitchen table across from Cass. "No girlfriend?"

Cass snorted and shook her head.

"Why not?"

"You know why."

"No, I don't," she said, shaking her head and reaching across the table to cover Cass's hand. "You've said the same thing to me before, and I pretended to understand, but I didn't. Not then, and I still don't now. Will you please tell me why?"

Cass just looked at her in disbelief. How could she not remember? Cass really didn't feel like going into it this early in the day. Hell, she didn't even know for sure she wasn't still sound asleep and dreaming all of this.

"Does Danny know you're here?"

"No. I wanted to surprise them. I decided at the last minute to book a flight and didn't have time to let anyone know anyway."

"They'll be surprised, trust me." Cass started to get up when the coffee was done brewing, but her mother waved her off and went to get it for them.

"Just sugar, right?"

"Yeah." Cass was surprised she remembered how she took her coffee but couldn't recall telling Cass to avoid getting trapped in a relationship. Funny how a person's mind worked.

"That didn't sound like a good *they'll be surprised* comment."

"They'll be thrilled to see you," Cass assured her before taking a sip from her mug. "But you need to know Judy's here too."

"When did she show up?"

Cass smiled at the fact her mother didn't even try to hide the animosity she felt for Barb's mother. There was no love lost between the two of them, and anyone who was acquainted with both of them knew it.

"Yesterday, but I'm pretty sure she's leaving today."

"Why such a short trip? I know she hates to fly, so driving from Virginia to stay one night seems odd, even for Judy."

"She took things a little too far with Danny last night," Cass told her, shifting uncomfortably in her chair. "She threatened to force Barb and the baby to go home with her. She hates the baby's name, and she isn't happy about the dyke aunt living so close by either."

"Are you serious?" her mother asked. Cass could tell her mother was fighting with herself to keep her temper under control. "She has the gall to not show up at her own daughter's wedding, and then she tries to pull this fucked up bullshit?"

Cass knew her mouth was hanging open. In all of her thirty-four years, she'd never heard her mother use language any stronger than *shit*, and even then it had only been one or two times. Hearing the f-word come out of her mother's mouth shocked Cass, and she wasn't even trying to hide it.

"If I said those words you'd wash my mouth out with soap."

"You really want to try it?"

Cass shook her head vigorously and turned her attention to the coffee she was gripping between her hands. She heard her mother chuckle, but Cass didn't look up. She was on the verge of laughing herself, and she knew if she met her mother's eyes she wouldn't be able to stop it.

"I take it Barb told her what she could do with that particular idea?"

"Barb was upstairs with the baby at the time. Danny, Erica, and I gave her a piece of our collective minds."

Oh, how Cass wanted those words back the very second they'd left her mouth. She looked up and caught her mother's surprised expression. Cass watched as she tilted her head to one side and studied her intently.

"Who's Erica?"

"A friend," Cass answered a little too quickly. She shook her head as her mother leaned forward, a sly grin forming.

"Of yours, or Barb's?"

"Mine."

Her mother waited silently for Cass to elaborate, but she refused to. If she thought Barb was trying to be a matchmaker, her mother was a thousand times worse. Cass sat there, her leg bouncing nervously. She reached down and patted Gordy on the head when she felt his body press up against her other leg.

"I'm starting to remember how much fun it is to get information out of you," her mother said with a frustrated sigh. "So, is she a friend, or is she a girlfriend?"

"She's a girl, and she's my friend." Cass tilted her head back and stared at the ceiling. Why did people always ask the very same question? "You have girlfriends, right? Why is it when I have friends who are girls, it means something different?"

"Because you're a lesbian," her mother answered as though it were obvious. It was, of course, but Cass was stalling for time. "Are you sleeping with her?"

"No," Cass answered, again a little too quickly.

"But you want to."

"I…" Cass started, but she didn't know how to respond. Yes, she wanted to, but this was her mother who was asking. Cass looked at her and saw the smug grin.

"That's why it's different, sweetie. I don't want to sleep with my female friends," she said, sitting back with a satisfied grin. "Now, tell me all about her."

"There's nothing to tell."

"I'm calling bullshit on that one."

"When did you start swearing so much?"

"I always have. Just not around you or your brother."

Cass shook her head and looked at Gordy, who still had his head resting on her thigh. She absently stroked the top of his head as he gazed up at her lovingly. Animals were so much easier to deal with than people. They never demanded you tell them all your feelings. Or about the woman you wanted to sleep with.

"Are you going to tell me about her, or am I going to have to ask Barb for all the juicy details?"

Chapter Fourteen

Cass spent the next hour telling her everything she knew about Erica while deftly dodging any questions she felt were getting too personal on the nature of their relationship. She figured it was better, and less embarrassing, coming from her than anyone else. When she went to refill her coffee mug, she noticed the kitchen light was on in the main house. Thank God. Maybe she could get her mother to go there for breakfast and give her a break from the inquisition.

She grabbed her phone and called the house. When Danny answered she breathed a sigh of relief. She only realized after hitting the call button it could very well be Judy who was up and about so early.

"Mom's here. Are you making breakfast?" she asked.

"I wasn't, but I can. Bring her on up. When did she get here?"

"A couple of hours ago," Cass said, even though it felt like longer. "I'll send her up and be along myself after a quick shower."

Cass hung up and turned back to her mother.

"You're kicking me out?" she asked.

"You must be hungry. Danny's cooking breakfast for you." Cass followed her to the door. "I'll bring your bags up when I come in a few minutes."

"My bags will stay right where they are," her mother said. She stopped with her hand on the doorknob and turned back to Cass. "If something's changed and Judy isn't leaving today, there's no way in hell I'm staying in the same house with her. The hostility would be too much for Barb and the baby to deal with."

Cass sighed. She should have known it was too good to be true. She nodded once in agreement, but her mother didn't move.

"What?" she asked, uncomfortable under the scrutiny.

"Don't think I've forgotten you never answered my question about why you never have a girlfriend." Her mother finally opened the door and stepped outside. "We *will* talk about it later."

Cass was so not looking forward to that conversation.

❖

After breakfast, Cass returned to her cabin and considered calling Erica. She hadn't given the PlayStation to Kyle the day before, but she still wanted him to have it as a thank you for all his help. She didn't know where things stood with Erica though, and the thought frightened her. Erica had been ready to sleep with her last night, but after Danny called, it was like a switch had been turned off. What if Erica never wanted to see her again? She knew the thought should have made her happy, but all she really felt was lost. She reached for her phone just before the front door opened and Gordy began barking.

"Don't you know how to knock?" she asked her mother as she shoved the phone into her pocket. Maybe she'd call Erica later. Or, even better, maybe Erica would call her.

"It was unlocked, dear. If you don't want someone walking in unannounced, you should lock it." She hung her coat on the hook by the door and removed her boots. "Judy is getting ready to leave, so I thought I'd give them some time to say good-bye."

Cass silently thanked whoever was responsible for Judy actually leaving. She realized then that she hadn't really believed she would go back home so soon. Cass watched her mother as she walked into the kitchen and filled a glass with water, Gordy following her with his tail wagging the whole time.

"The baby is so cute," her mother said with a slight smile. "And I can't believe they named him after my grandfather."

"It was Barb's idea. Danny wanted to name him after himself," Cass told her.

"Really?"

Cass shifted uncomfortably when she noticed her mother's eyes welling up with tears. She'd seen her mother cry plenty of times, usually because of something her father said or did, but it didn't make it any easier to deal with. Cass always found it unnerving when anyone cried.

"Well then, I love her even more," her mother said, wiping the tears away before they could spill out of her eyes. She looked at Cass and laughed. "I loved my grandfather dearly, but why on earth would someone name a baby Clarence in this day and age?"

Cass merely shrugged. It had been her first thought too, but she hadn't voiced her opinion. Barb seemed so happy to be naming him after someone in Danny's family instead of her own. Cass was pretty sure Barb only chose the name to piss Judy off. Mission accomplished.

"When are you going to give me grandchildren?"

"Mom," Cass said, shaking her head. She knew she couldn't avoid the subject forever, but her nerves were still on edge after Erica basically walked out on her while she was naked.

"Why, Cass? Why are you so against having a relationship?"

"You really don't know?"

"I wouldn't be asking if I did, would I?"

Cass took a deep breath. She found it hard to believe her mother could have forgotten what had been a watershed moment for Cass. The moment that had in turn shaped her entire adult life. She situated herself into the corner of the couch so she was facing her mother.

"You told me once—I think I must have been about fourteen at the time—you said you didn't want me to make the same mistakes you did. You said I should follow my dreams and not let anyone take them away from me." Cass watched as her mother's expression shifted slowly from confusion to understanding. "And you said I shouldn't allow myself to be tied down or have my spirit stifled."

"Oh, sweetie," her mother said, unable to stop the tears this time. "So you're saying I'm to blame for you never having a girlfriend?"

"I'm not blaming you, Mom. I blame Dad."

"Cass," her mother said, grabbing her hand and squeezing it gently. Cass waited as she was obviously trying to find the right words to express herself. She finally shook her head. "Baby, I didn't mean you shouldn't ever fall in love. Just because I found myself trapped in an unhealthy relationship doesn't mean *all* relationships are bad. My parents were married for over fifty years, and they loved each other immensely. I wish I'd had the fortune to find my soul mate back then, but I didn't. But it doesn't mean I don't believe in love. I've met a wonderful man who treats me like a queen, and I couldn't be happier."

"But Dad was awful to you. He forced you to stay home and raise his children." Cass was confused. She'd expected her mother to never even consider another relationship once her father was gone. "He wouldn't even let you have friends. He dictated every aspect of your life."

"You're right, he did. But I'm partly to blame for it, because I allowed him to have that kind of power over me. And you know what?" she asked, reaching out to cup Cass's chin. "I wouldn't change a second of it, because I have the two most wonderful children in the world. You and Danny are my life. I stayed with your father to protect the two of you. He threatened to kill you both if I ever walked out on him."

"You never told me."

"There was no reason for you to know. I wasn't going to do anything to put either of you at risk. I knew he'd never touch you or Danny as long as I stayed with him, so I did what I had to do in order to protect you." She let go of Cass's hand and wiped the tears off her cheeks. "Luckily, there are more good people in the world than bad. You're father's dead, and I can't honestly say I'm sorry he's gone. You can't allow him to dictate your life, Cassidy. You loving another human being would be the best *fuck you* you could ever hope to give him."

Cass tried to smile, because deep down she knew her mother was right. But her father's words kept replaying over and over in her mind. Her distress must have been written all over her face, because her mother knew there was something more.

"What else?"

Cass couldn't meet her mother's eyes. She'd never told anyone, not even Danny about the things their father had said to her. After a few moments, she looked at her mother.

"He told me I was worthless, and no one could ever love me. That the only thing women were good for was catering to their husband's every whim. And having babies. Can't forget that one."

"I swear to God, if he were still alive, I'd kill him," her mother said. She grabbed Cass's hand again and held it tightly. "You have to know those things aren't true, sweetie. He was nothing but a misogynistic asshole. You are so worthy of love, and you will find it someday."

Cass sat there motionless. She wasn't sure she could move even if she'd wanted to. Maybe she was in shock. Maybe she was only now realizing she could actually have a girlfriend and allow herself to be happy. Maybe Erica would be willing to be that girlfriend. Or, maybe Erica had washed her hands of anything to do with her. Cass swallowed and looked down at her shaking hands.

"Have you ever loved anyone, Cassidy?"

"No."

"Was it because you wouldn't let yourself, or because you just haven't found the right woman yet?" her mother asked.

"Probably a little of both," Cass admitted.

"What about Erica?"

"I think I could love her, maybe, if the fates are on my side."

"We make our own fate, darling, and don't you ever forget that."

Cass smiled and nodded, hoping it would be easy to break herself out of the habits she'd grown so accustomed to over the years. She'd spent so long avoiding getting close to anyone, what if she couldn't let go enough to even give herself the chance?

CHAPTER FIFTEEN

Erica woke that morning after having spent the better part of the night tossing and turning. Sleep was triumphant in eluding her, and successful in mocking her endlessly. On the few occasions when she was able to drift off, it was only to dream about Cass standing before her, completely naked.

"Jesus Christ, did I really walk out on naked Cass?" she murmured, causing Willie to open his eyes and yawn. Well, good, at least he'd been able to sleep. She stared at the ceiling, unable to get the visual out of her head, even now. Cass had an exquisite body. The perfect combination of strength and beauty. Her breasts were firm, her arms strong, and her stomach flat. Erica admitted to herself she'd never seen anyone more gorgeous. And yes, she *had* walked out on naked Cass. "I'm a fool."

She covered her face with her pillow when she thought about what might have happened next, had Danny not called. His timing definitely sucked. She groaned and held the pillow tightly against her face, not wanting Kyle to hear her and worry something was wrong. She peeked at the bedside clock, surprised to see it was only eight o'clock. She wondered if Cass would be up yet. It was Sunday after all.

After sitting up and tucking the pillow behind her back, she grabbed the phone from where it resided next to the clock and scrolled through her contacts until she found Cass. She was about to tap the button to place the call when she realized how stupid she was being. What could she possibly say to make things right between them?

No, it was probably better to maintain some distance from Cass for a while. They weren't looking for the same things, a fact made crystal clear the night before. She refused to get involved with anyone who didn't have an eye to the future, and it was obvious Cass only lived in the moment. Their two worlds could never come together. She'd known her what? A week? Two? What did it matter, really? Time to pick herself up and dust herself off. Keep on keepin' on. Keep moving and don't look back.

She groaned.

She pulled her legs up so her heels were touching her butt and rested her forehead on her knees. She never realized before how epically bad she was at giving herself pep talks.

Of course, it might be a whole lot easier if naked Cass wasn't permanently imprinted on her brain. She'd just made up her mind to make her way to the kitchen and fix something for breakfast when her phone rang. She picked it up and looked at it.

"Shit," she said when she saw *Cassidy Holmes* on the caller ID. Hadn't she just decided it would be best not to talk to her? After taking a deep breath, she answered. "Hello?"

"Erica?" she said, her silky smooth voice causing goose bumps on Erica's arms. "It's Cass. I didn't wake you, did I?"

"No," she said, trying her best to sound cheery. Kind of hard to do when I didn't even sleep, she thought, but barely stopped herself from saying out loud.

"Good." Cass sounded relieved. And well rested, damn her. "Listen, I had something I wanted to give to Kyle, and I completely forgot about it last night. I thought it would be better to call rather than just show up there out of the blue."

"You don't need to give him anything, Cass. He was happy to help you yesterday."

"Yeah? You think he'd be interested in doing it again sometime?" Cass sounded hopeful, and for a second, Erica wondered if she was really talking about Kyle. "He was a big help, and you were too. But I'd really like to give him something for his time."

Of course she did. That was just the person Cass was. But really, what could it hurt? Yes, Kyle had been excited about helping Cass, and she was sure he didn't expect anything in return, but if it made Cass feel better, why not?

"Okay," she said after a moment.

"Great. Is it all right if I drop by this afternoon?"

"Sure."

"Cool."

"Yep."

For God's sake, how long could this inane one word at a time conversation go on? Erica was about to tell her good-bye when Cass spoke again, and when she heard her voice, Erica couldn't hang up.

"Erica?"

How was it possible for someone to put so much meaning into a simple name? Cass sounded desperate and unsure, yet confident and cool all at the same time. Erica was going to have to work on that vibe for herself. It was incredibly sexy.

"What?"

"I'm sorry about last night."

Really? Cass was the one who was apologizing? How ludicrous was that? Erica was the one who ran away, practically leaving naked Cass standing there in the living room all alone. She knew she had to say something in response, but her tongue picked the most inopportune time to decide to stop working properly.

"I'll see you later," Cass said just before disconnecting the call.

Erica sat there for a few minutes, wondering what the hell had just happened. This was not acceptable. She was the one who needed to apologize, not Cass. And she would do just that when Cass came by later.

❖

"Why do I have the feeling your conversation didn't go as well as you thought it might?" Danny asked. Judy had finally left to drive back to Virginia, and their mother was making herself comfortable in the room she'd vacated.

"Probably because it didn't." Cass shrugged in an attempt to convey it was no big deal, but her brother knew her too well to fall for the cavalier attitude.

"You'll talk to her when you go over there later and work things out, right?"

"There isn't anything to work out, Daniel," she said, knowing how much he hated being addressed by his given name. It had been their father's name, and as soon as Danny had reached an age where he understood what a prick their old man was, he insisted on being called Danny. Anything to distance himself, right? Which was why Cass had been surprised he'd even entertained naming the baby Daniel too.

"She's looking for forever, and I'm not. Does that sound like something we can work out?"

"You never know until you try, right?"

"She deserves more. She deserves someone who isn't going to *try,* but who's committed to making it work." Damn it, what didn't he get about this? Yes, she'd wavered in her own mind, and had even seriously considered it after the talk with her mother earlier. But she'd never said out loud what she was thinking. And more importantly, she'd come to her senses and realized it would probably never work.

"You could be that person, Cass, and you damn well know it," Barb said as she walked into the kitchen. Cass wondered how long she'd been standing outside the door listening, but didn't give voice to the question. Cass watched in silence as Barb poured herself a cup of coffee then refilled Cass's cup.

"I'm sorry about what happened with your mother last night," Danny said with a quick kiss to his wife's cheek.

"I'm not," Cass chipped in. When Barb shot a glance her way, Cass shrugged. "What? Okay, I'm sorry because I'm not sorry about what happened last night. Better?"

Barb shook her head, but Cass saw the amusement in her eyes. Cass tried not to smile as she lifted a cup filled with fresh coffee to her lips. Barb leaned a hip against the counter but didn't look away from her.

"My mother said, and I quote, *Cassidy's dyke girlfriend got in my face*," Barb said, waiting for some kind of response, no doubt. Cass just watched her. "I told her by implying Erica was your girlfriend, it would be assumed she was a dyke, and therefore her statement was redundant. She wasn't amused, because she thought she was using the word as an insult."

"Erica is not my girlfriend." Cass hoped her tone indicated the subject was closed, but this was Barb she was talking to. Barb was the queen of getting in the last word. She was just happy no one had brought all this up during breakfast with Judy and her mother both sitting at the same table.

"You could have fooled me." Barb took a sip of her coffee, and Cass took the opportunity to look at Danny, pleading with her eyes for him to rescue her. The coward turned away from them and poured himself a cup of coffee. "Because the way you two look at each other borders on scandalous."

"Yeah, well, lust and love are two very different things," Cass said, setting her cup down.

"So it's just lust?"

Cass started to answer, but she closed her mouth and shook her head. Damn it. It wasn't just lust, but there was no way she was going to admit it to Barb. She also wasn't about to admit, even to herself, that she was feeling more for Erica than she ever had for anyone before. And no matter what she did, she couldn't stop thinking about Erica. She hoped the flush she felt warm her cheeks at the image of her stripped naked in front of a fully clothed Erica wasn't visible.

"Ha! I knew it was more than lust," Barb said. She smirked before pushing away from the counter and walking over to take a seat at the table with Cass. She lowered her voice, and Cass was grateful because she really didn't want to be having this conversation in front of her brother. Or her mother, who could very well come walking in at any moment. Barb placed a hand gently on Cass's forearm. "Love is precious, Cass."

"I haven't known her long enough to be in love," Cass said.

"Is there a handbook I'm not aware of that states you have to know someone a certain length of time before realizing you love them?" Barb squeezed her forearm. "When you find it, you have to hold on to it with both hands. Because," she glanced over her shoulder and smiled at Danny, who still had his back to them, "things might get tough at times, but it is so worth it."

Cass sighed. She was tired of everyone trying to tell her she needed to find someone to settle down with. If there was anyone she wanted forever with, it would be Erica, but...*what the hell?* Where had that thought come from?

"You look like you just had an epiphany," Barb said, looking proud of herself.

"More like a wake-up call," Cass answered. She stood and grabbed the jacket she'd hung on the back of her chair. The look on Barb's face stopped her from explaining, but she probably wouldn't have anyway. The "epiphany" she'd had wasn't what Barb thought. It was simply the realization she'd let her defenses down, and Erica had managed to find her way in. All she had to do now was distance herself from the situation, and she'd feel like her old self again. Cass kissed Barb on the cheek and said her good-byes before rushing out the door.

CHAPTER SIXTEEN

Cass pulled her car over on the side of the road three houses away from Erica's. Her heart was racing, and she couldn't get it to slow down. What if she was having a heart attack? She chuckled at the thought and pressed her forehead against the steering wheel. She knew it wasn't funny, but it was easier to laugh at herself than admit she might be having a panic attack.

When she'd pulled out of her driveway, she'd been resolute. No matter what her mother had said earlier, she was going to tell Erica there was nowhere for their relationship to go. It's not you; it's me. How cliché, and Cass figured Erica was smart enough to see right through it. With every mile she got closer to Erica's, the more she felt her resolve slipping. She knew if she were to find herself alone with Erica, she wouldn't be able to stand firm in her decision.

And she had to. It would never work out between them because they wanted different things out of life. It wasn't as if she could change the way she'd lived her entire thirty-four years in a matter of hours. Cass would be thrilled if Erica decided to go the friends with benefits route, but she wasn't holding out much hope on that particular front. Maybe Cass *could* make it work. As long as Erica knew from the beginning how she felt…

She lifted her head slightly and banged it against the steering wheel. Was she really willing to do that just to get a woman into bed? No. She could drive to Buffalo or Rochester right now and hook up with almost any woman she wanted. The thought exhilarated her, but when she thought about it, *really* thought about it, the desire wasn't there. What the hell was happening to her?

She jumped and whipped her head away from the steering wheel when she heard someone knock on the window. She looked over to see Kyle peering in at her. He waved a gloved hand and looked way too cheerful with the goofy grin he was sporting. Cass shook her head and tried to look pissed off as she pushed the button to lower the window.

"Are you trying to scare the living hell out of me?" she asked.

"Sorry," he said, looking concerned. "I thought maybe there was something wrong. I just wanted to make sure you were okay. Are you? Okay, I mean."

"I'm fine. What are you doing out here anyway?"

"Erica sent me out to shovel the driveway because you were coming over." Kyle straightened and leaned against the snow shovel Cass hadn't noticed he was holding. "So you better pull in because I don't want to have spent the past hour doing this for nothing."

His tone was playful, but his look stern. Cass imagined he didn't know quite how to feel at her gruff greeting, and she felt bad. There was no reason to take her foul mood out on him. He'd been nothing but nice to her since the day she'd delivered him to Erica's doorstep.

"I'm sorry," she said. "Get in and I'll give you a ride."

"It's three houses from here," he said with a slight grin that made Cass think he was wondering if she'd lost her mind.

Maybe she had. She had a feeling it would be easier than stressing over whether she could actually make a real relationship work.

"Smartass." She put the car in gear and started to go, but he put a hand on the door so she'd stop. She couldn't handle the look of concern on his face. He was too young to be as insightful as he came across.

"Are you sure you're okay?"

"I'm sure, Kyle," she said with a nod. She pasted a smile on her face, hoping to convince him she didn't have a care in the world, even though she felt like her life was spinning out of control. "But thank you for your concern. You're a good kid. Now get home because I brought something for you."

"Cool. I'll be right there," he said, holding the shovel up. "I just have to return this to the old lady down the street. I had to promise to shovel her driveway before she'd let me use it."

Cass laughed as she watched him take off in the opposite direction of Erica's house. She sobered quickly when she realized it meant she'd be alone with Erica.

She could do this.

Right?

❖

Erica pulled the door open, expecting to see Kyle since he'd left her keys there when he went to borrow a shovel. She inhaled sharply at the sight of Cass standing on her porch. She stood there motionless for a moment, their eyes locking, and all reason fleeing her mind. She wanted to open the screen door, grab Cass by the hand, and drag her through the house to her bedroom in the back. Instead, she opened the screen door and motioned for her to come in.

"Is that a PlayStation?" Erica asked, indicating the machine Cass held in her arms.

"It is," Cass replied. She went to the entertainment center in the corner and set it on the floor. "Kyle seemed excited when he saw it in the stuff we pulled out of the unit yesterday. I thought he might like it."

"He would like it, very much, but it's not necessary, Cass," Erica said. She left the door open an inch or two so Kyle knew he could get in without knocking before going to sit on the couch. "He doesn't need it."

"Nobody *needs* a gaming system, Erica." Cass smiled and sat at the other end of the couch. "I'd keep it myself, but I already have one, and so does Danny."

"You could sell it."

Cass nodded and looked at the console she'd placed on the floor. "I could, but people want the PS4 now. The PS3 will be pretty much obsolete in a few years, which means I probably wouldn't be able to get much for it. I brought some games too. I know Kyle will get a lot of use out of it, and he can take it with him when he goes back home."

Erica didn't know what to say. It was unusual for anyone to offer a gift to someone they didn't really know, wasn't it? Kyle was enthralled with Cass, that much was obvious, and so was she if she was being honest. Which, of course, only made it harder for her to say no to Cass.

"I'm looking into getting guardianship of Kyle," she said after a moment. Cass looked at her, the surprise evident in her eyes. Erica was truly amazed herself. She hadn't intended to tell Cass about it. Or anyone, really. But it was done now, so she forced herself to continue. "It's not like our parents want him back. They've made that perfectly clear. I just haven't talked to him about it yet."

"You think he'll object?"

"No, but it doesn't mean he won't be hurt because of the reasons why it's happening." Erica stared at a picture of Kyle hanging on the wall. It was taken on his fifth birthday, and life had been perfect for both of them at the time. If she'd only known how quickly things would fall apart just a few years later. "Damn it, how can they do this to him? Parents are supposed to protect their children, aren't they?"

Erica swiped angrily at the tears running down her cheeks, and the next thing she knew, Cass was by her side, holding her while she cried. She knew she should pull away, but the strength Cass offered felt so safe and warm. She buried her face against Cass's neck and let the tears fall.

"You're going to be an awesome guardian for him, Erica," Cass said. "It's obvious how much he loves you, and you him. He'll thrive with you to guide him, I just know it."

Erica pulled back so she could look into Cass's eyes. She expected to see compassion there, but she really wasn't prepared for the magnitude of it. When Cass glanced quickly at her lips, Erica ran a hand through Cass's hair, stopping to cradle her cheek. Cass leaned into her touch and closed her eyes, and Erica thought she'd never seen anything more beautiful in her life. Without thinking, she leaned in and pressed her forehead to hers. She wanted nothing more than to kiss her, but she wasn't entirely sure it would be welcome.

"We should talk about last night," she said. Her breath hitched when Cass looked at her. "I'm not sure where we left things."

"I was naked, and you weren't," Cass answered, a glint in her eye. Erica tried not to react when Cass ran a hand up her side and cupped her breast, squeezing gently. "I feel like I'm at a disadvantage now."

"On the contrary," Erica said, enjoying the delicious hum starting deep in her core. She fought to maintain control of herself. "My seeing you naked gives you a huge advantage."

"Yeah?" Cass pinched a nipple through her clothes that Erica felt all the way to her toes.

"An enormous advantage." Erica nodded. "I can't even explain how much of an advantage you have now."

"Good to know."

"Oh, holy hell," Kyle said, sounding embarrassed.

Erica jumped when she heard the words at the same time she heard the screen door open. She moved away from Cass, who looked as dazed as Erica felt. Kyle stood there staring at them for a moment before shaking his head and smiling.

"Really? You want to pretend I didn't just walk in here and see you practically crawling into Cass's lap?" He laughed and walked into the kitchen. "I'm not six, you know. I'm well aware of what two people who are attracted to each other do when they're alone."

Erica glared at Cass, who had started laughing and tried to cover it with a cough. Erica didn't fail to see the humor in the situation, but she felt she needed to display some kind of parental authority. Kyle placed a hand on her shoulder when he came back into the living room.

"But you do realize you have a bedroom, right? I mean, you could shut the door and I'd be smart enough not to just open it without knocking first." He cocked his head to one side and raised his eyebrows at her. "And it's way down at the other end of the trailer, so I'd probably never even hear anything."

"Okay, enough," Erica said, trying to sound stern but failing when Cass finally laughed out loud. She slapped Cass on the thigh. "And you aren't helping here, you know."

"I'm sorry," Cass said. She ran a hand over her face and was all serious then. "Has anyone ever told you you're cute when you blush?"

Erica felt the heat rise and she buried her head in her hands, admitting she was fighting a losing battle. Cass and Kyle seemed to feed off each other, and while in this instance it was a little annoying, she was exponentially happy because Kyle *was* able to laugh.

"What the…" Kyle said. Erica glanced up in time to see him give Cass a questioning look before pointing at the gaming console on the floor. "What's this?"

"What do you think it is?" Cass asked.

"I think it's a PS3, but why is it here?"

"It's for you. For helping me so much yesterday."

"Are you sure?" Kyle looked skeptical, and when he turned his attention to Erica, she nodded to him. "I don't know what to say. My parents…"

Erica's heart broke when she saw him look away and wipe the tears from his eyes. He wasn't stupid, and she knew he had to be wondering what was going to happen to him. She needed to sit him down and discuss her plan with him. He deserved to have a say in his future.

"My parents wouldn't let me get one," he finally said when he faced them again. "Thank you so much, Cass. I really mean it."

"I can tell you do," Cass said. "And you're very welcome. And I was hoping you might want to help me again sometime. If it's okay with your sister."

"It's more than okay," Erica said. She didn't pull away when Cass took her hand and held it tightly. Even if things would never work out between them, she couldn't deny Kyle being friends with her. Cassidy Holmes was a good person, and Kyle needed more of those in his life. Now more than ever.

Chapter Seventeen

Cass played games with Kyle for the rest of the afternoon. She hadn't intended to spend all day there, but when he asked, and Erica told her she was more than welcome, she realized she didn't want to be anywhere else. The thought scared her for a few moments, especially after remembering Erica telling her she was looking into being Kyle's legal guardian. The thought she couldn't change her entire life based on a single conversation with her mother was still fresh in her mind.

Cass wasn't entirely sure she wanted a relationship, much less a ready-made family. He'd never said anything, but she was sure Danny was feeling the pressure to get a real job now since there was another mouth to feed, and Cass had absolutely no desire to find a real job. The one and only job she'd had working for someone else had been in high school. Burger King. She hated it. With a passion.

Why anyone would want to work for someone else was beyond her. Being at the mercy of a boss to tell you when you had to be there, when you could leave, what days you got off, sucked. Big time. She only lasted a couple of weeks there before she told the manager where he could shove his schedule.

Cass had gone with her best friend, Nora, and Nora's father, to a storage auction a couple of times, and she told her mother that was what she wanted to do. Her mother, unbeknownst to her father, had scrimped and saved all she could for months before handing Cass an envelope containing a thousand dollars on the day she graduated from high school. It was the best day of her teenage life.

She'd bought her first unit for three hundred dollars, made an eight hundred dollar profit, and never looked back. Danny helped her after school and on weekends, and when he graduated, their mother had done the same for him. Cass didn't know what their father's reaction to it had been, but she knew her mother steered clear of him for a long time after.

"Football or baseball?" Kyle asked as he grabbed the games and looked through them for what had to be the twelfth time. They'd just spent the past three hours playing *Resistance: Fall of Man*, and Cass didn't want to admit to him her thumbs hurt from pressing buttons and moving the joystick.

"Why don't you guys take a break?" Erica called from the kitchen.

Cass looked at her and smiled her thanks just as the aroma of something wonderful made its presence known to her. How had she not noticed it before? It smelled a lot like the meatloaf her mother used to make because it was Cass's favorite meal. She stood from where she'd been sitting on the floor and stretched, not realizing how uncomfortable she'd really been. She winced when she felt something pop in her back.

"Getting old?" Kyle asked, and she pushed him with her foot. He laughed and just continued playing a game on his own.

Cass walked into the kitchen and leaned against the counter in order to watch Erica cook. Her mother had always set her on the counter so she could watch, and she'd never outgrown the need to observe while someone else was preparing a meal. She should have learned by osmosis how to cook herself, but alas, she could heat a can of soup, but anything more complicated was pretty much impossible.

"What?" Erica asked, obviously feeling uncomfortable under her scrutiny. "Am I doing something wrong?"

"I wouldn't know." Cass shrugged and smiled. "I just like to watch."

"A cooking voyeur?" Erica laughed and shook her head as she went back to cutting up vegetables.

"Too kinky for you?"

Erica stopped what she was doing and looked at her. Cass wanted to look away, but she couldn't. She took the knife out of Erica's grasp and held her hand, bringing it to her lips. She watched as Erica's eyes darkened.

"I'm sorry about last night," Cass said. She placed a finger over Erica's lips when it looked as if she were going to respond. She had to say what was on her mind without interruption. "You are the most interesting woman I've ever met. I want to be with you, but I'm afraid I can't give you what you need. I've been alone for so long, never even wanting more than a night with any one woman, I wouldn't even know how to act in a relationship."

"Then don't," Erica said.

"What?" Cass asked, confused.

"Don't act. Just be yourself."

"But that's the point," Cass said. "I'm not sure being myself would be enough for you. You deserve so much more."

"How can you know you wouldn't be enough unless you try?"

Cass stared down at her feet, wondering why someone like Erica would want her so much that she would try this hard to convince her it could work. It wasn't even like they knew each other very well. A part of her wanted to try, but the other part, the *bigger* part, knew she'd end up disappointing Erica, which was the last thing she wanted. But how could she make Erica understand?

"Stay for dinner?" Erica asked, causing Cass to meet her eyes again. Erica shrugged like it was no big deal, and picked up the knife again. "We can still be friends, right? I understand it'll never be any more, Cass, but you sell and ship the things you buy in those storage units, so we're going to be seeing each other. A lot, probably. Besides, your brother gave me this recipe last night because he said it was your favorite meal."

"So you're making this for me?"

"Yes, I guess I am."

"Then how can I say no?" Cass grinned, but her heart hurt. It actually *hurt*. Whether it was because she didn't like the fact Erica gave up so easily or if it was because she seemed to just accept there'd never be anything but friendship in their future, she wasn't sure.

But Cass had a feeling it was simply because she herself wanted more, wanted to try, but she'd succeeded in pushing Erica away, and therefore sealed her fate. She'd be alone forever. Which was what she wanted, right?

❖

"That was so good," Cass said, having reached her limit after her third helping of meatloaf. She pushed her plate away and sat back, her hands over her belly. "I shouldn't have had that last piece."

"I tried to tell you," Erica said.

"We both did," Kyle added. "But you're stubborn."

"I am not." Cass tried to sound offended, but the grin on Kyle's face made it impossible.

"You are," Erica said. She stood and stacked everyone's plates to take them to the sink. She looked at Kyle. "You get to do the dishes tonight."

"Aw, sis, come on," he said as he followed her to the kitchen. "I wanted to play some more games."

"You can play after I go to bed, as long as you're quiet."

Cass smiled at the bickering because it reminded her of her and Danny when they were young. Hell, it reminded her of how they were now. She was just getting up from the table when Erica brought her a cup of coffee. She motioned with her head for Cass to follow her to the couch.

"Did you want cream or sugar?"

"Sugar would be great," Cass answered, sitting so they were a couple feet apart. She was afraid she'd need to touch her if she sat too close. She put a teaspoon of sugar in her coffee from the container Erica set on the table. "Thank you. Dinner was wonderful, by the way."

"Like I couldn't tell by how much you ate." Erica smiled. "Thank you."

They sat in silence, and Cass really wasn't sure what they should talk about. She wanted to kiss Erica, but she was pretty sure such a move wouldn't be welcome from someone who was just a friend. She'd never had many friends who were girls before. She had plenty of guy friends, but this was uncharted territory for her. Was it even possible to be friends with someone you were so incredibly attracted to?

"You told Kyle he could play after you went to bed," she said in an attempt to end the uncomfortable quiet. "You go to bed earlier than he does?"

"I go to bed at eight when I have to work the next day."

"Why so early?"

"I get up at four, so if I want eight hours, I have to get to bed early."

"That seems crazy."

"It does, but it's the job I accepted. I work six to two thirty." Erica placed her cup on the coffee table and rested her hands on her thighs. "It's not always easy, especially since you showed up with Kyle on my doorstep, but it is what it is."

"But you have weekends off? I guess that's a nice perk."

"I have every other Saturday off. I had this weekend, but next week my days off will be Sunday and Monday," Erica said.

"That sucks," Cass said. She held her cup tightly in her hands so she could resist the temptation of touching Erica. This just being friends thing was going to be difficult.

"It isn't so bad. It's so much better than where I was in Syracuse. I knew if I didn't get away from all the drama it would've only been a matter of time before my head exploded. Dating among coworkers runs rampant at the post office. And it inevitably turns out bad not only for the two people involved, but for the people who have to work with them too."

"I take it you dated a coworker?" Cass really didn't want to hear about it, but wasn't this what friends did for each other? Listen to the horror stories of their past?

"God, no," Erica said. She laughed and reached for Cass's leg, but she must have thought better of it because she pulled her hand back at the last possible moment. "There wasn't anyone there I found interesting enough to see outside of work."

Cass didn't understand the relief she felt at the statement. Why should she care who Erica dated in the past? These feelings were confusing, and she didn't like it at all. Not one bit. She should leave before she did something, or said something, she'd regret. She put her cup down and got to her feet.

"I should probably go," she said, watching as Erica stood too. When Erica took a step toward her, Cass didn't move. She closed her eyes momentarily and tried to find her resolve, but it was elusive. When she opened her eyes again, Erica was looking at her lips. She had to think of something to say to break the spell. "You have to go to bed soon, right?"

Shit, that was so not the thing to say. Erica met her eyes and smiled, and Cass felt her knees go weak. Wait, what? These kinds of things did not happen to Cassidy Holmes. Ever. She forced herself to take a step backward, but Erica moved with her. The need to kiss Erica was overwhelming, and when Erica reached for her, Cass didn't resist.

"What happened to being friends?" Erica asked when Cass put her hands on her hips to pull her closer.

"We can be friends," Cass said. "Can't we? Is it against the friends rules to kiss?"

"I don't think there are any rules," Erica answered just before she covered Cass's mouth with her own.

Cass sighed in relief and let Erica take charge. She'd never given up control before, but it felt right somehow. With Erica it was definitely right. The thought sobered her, and she pulled away quickly, causing a whimper from Erica. The sound sent a jolt of electricity through Cass. She shook her head and backed away toward the door.

"I can't do this. I'm so sorry," she said before practically running out. The last vision of Erica in her mind was her standing by the couch with a bewildered look on her face. It wasn't fair to Erica that she left the way she did, but it was what had to be done. Cass simply could not think straight when she was in her presence.

Chapter Eighteen

Erica stood there, dumbfounded, staring at the door long after Cass walked out. She couldn't believe one minute they were kissing like lovers, and the next she was gone. How the hell did someone walk away from such a kiss? She knew Cass was into it too, that it wasn't only her who was enjoying the kiss.

"She left?" Kyle asked as he walked out of the kitchen.

Erica just looked at him, not knowing what to say. His shoulders sagged and he gave her a look of disappointment. He looked so much like their father right then, and she almost cried for everything they'd both lost.

"What did you do?"

"Excuse me?"

"What did you do to scare her away?"

"Come sit down," Erica said. She settled in on the couch and patted the cushion next to her. He did as she asked, but he looked sullen. He reminded her of someone who'd just lost their puppy. It was strange for him to look one minute so much like their father, and then in the next to seem like a little boy. She shook it off and let out a frustrated sigh. "We want different things out of life, Kyle. She doesn't want forever."

She watched him in silence as he appeared to be considering her words. Twice he started to say something, but then he'd shake his head and look away from her. She wanted to let him give her a response without prompting, so she continued to wait.

"I can kind of understand her point," he finally said, his eyes focused on some spot on the wall Erica couldn't see. "Forever is a pretty scary concept if you really think about it. But I guess if it's what *you* want, it wouldn't seem daunting to you."

"Tell me why you think it's scary. Isn't it what you want too?"

"Maybe someday, but I'm not even sixteen yet, Erica." He looked at her like she was crazy, and she laughed. Of course the thought of forever would sound terrifying to someone his age.

"But she's around my age," Erica pointed out. "Most people my age are looking to settle down. Start a family."

"Really? You actually know most people your age? You can't speak for everyone."

"You're right. I could be wrong, but I know it's what I want."

"And what does she want?"

She opened her mouth to answer him, but thought better of it in the nick of time. What could she say? Cass wants a one-night stand? She wants a friends with benefits scenario? No, it might be hard for Erica to remember Kyle wasn't older than he was because he was so well read and articulate, but he *was* still a child.

"I'm not sure, but I know it isn't anything long-term." Erica thought about how Cass kissed her and wondered if it was really true. "Mostly, she wants to be friends."

"Bull," Kyle said, waving a hand at her dismissively. "Saying that's usually the kiss of death for kids my age, but I think she wants to spend time with you, and it's easier to lie than to admit she wants more. You need to make her see she wants more."

"No, Kyle. If she's not interested, I'm not going to beg. I will not be that woman who continuously throws herself at someone who has no interest."

"But she is interested," Kyle said with a nod. He seemed so sure of himself, but Erica shook her head.

"I have to take what she says at face value, Kyle," she said, knowing it was true, but wanting so much to believe Cass might change her mind if they spent more time together. "I don't know her well enough to be able to read between the lines, so I have to trust she would tell me if she wanted more."

"You have so much to learn about women." Kyle snorted, and it caused them both to start laughing uncontrollably.

She missed spending time like this with him, but then again, it looked as if they were going to have a lot of nights in their future to sit and talk. She put her arms around her middle and tried hard to stop laughing. She'd almost accomplish it, and then he'd start up again. When they finally wore themselves out, they both wiped the tears from their cheeks. Erica glanced at the clock and knew she should get to bed. Four a.m. came awfully early.

"What's going to happen to me?"

"What do you mean?" Erica was concerned, and she knew it was obvious in her tone. He was sad, and he looked like he was going to cry, but he clenched his teeth and it looked to Erica like he wasn't going to allow it to happen just by sheer will power. She brushed the bangs from his forehead and forced a smile. "You need a haircut."

"So do you." He gave her a small smile before looking away. "I can't go home because they made their feelings pretty clear. I can't ask you to let me live here until I graduate high school, because you don't need that right now. So what's going to happen to me?"

Erica swallowed the lump in her throat and ignored the ache in her chest his words had caused. Did he really think she would turn away from him too? She hadn't been the best sister to him since her coming out incident, but she vowed to make up for her shortcomings.

"Nothing's going to happen to you," she told him. He still refused to look at her, but she went on, hoping her words would resonate with him. "I would never let you become homeless. And I will not let you go into the foster system. I'm your sister, and I would never let anything bad happen to you. You know that, right?"

"Yes."

"Would you be open to the possibility of living here with me? Permanently?"

He finally looked at her, and she waited, holding her breath, for his response.

"I can't ask you to do that," he said, his voice almost a whisper.

"You didn't."

"Are you sure? I mean, I know teenagers can be a handful sometimes."

"You're a good kid, Kyle. We'll be okay."

"Then what do we need to do?"

"I already spoke with an attorney, and we're working on getting me declared your legal guardian." She couldn't contain her smile when she saw how excited he was at the prospect. The energy coming off him was almost palpable. "We'll need to get you enrolled in high school here."

"When?"

"I'll come pick you up after work tomorrow and we'll drive over there then, all right?"

"Thank you," he said just before he engulfed her in a big hug. She felt his tears on her own cheek and she squeezed him briefly. "I love you."

"I love you, too," she said when Kyle pulled away from her. "I need to get to bed. You'll be all right?"

"Yeah. I'll see you tomorrow."

CHAPTER NINETEEN

Cass entered her brother's house without knocking because the lights were on. If they hadn't been, she would have just gone home and gone to bed, even though she knew she wouldn't sleep any more tonight than she had the night before.

"Didn't expect to see you home tonight," Barb said when she walked into the living room where they were watching television. "Danny said you were going to Erica's."

"I was there, but now I'm here."

"Ooh, cryptic," Barb said before hitting Danny in the thigh with the back of her hand. "You should find something to do upstairs. Like check on the baby or something. We need to have some girl talk."

"Can you even have girl talk with a lesbian?" Danny grinned, but his comment only earned him another shot in the leg, but this time with a closed fist and more force behind it. "Ouch. All I meant was—"

"Do yourself a favor and don't say anything more," Cass said. She didn't really care. She was used to the guys around town treating her like one of them. Barb, on the other hand, had appointed herself protector of all things lesbian. Cass admitted to herself it was pretty nice to have someone stick up for her in these situations.

He glared at them both, no doubt trying to think up ways to get back at them, but without another word, he turned and went up the stairs. He didn't even try to be quiet.

"You wake the baby and you're dealing with him on your own, Daniel," Barb called after him. Her smile conveyed the satisfaction she felt when they heard Danny mumble something and then there was silence. Barb leaned forward and put a hand on Cass's knee.

"Is Mom in bed?" Cass asked, hoping to forestall whatever conversation Barb had in her mind they were going to have.

"Yes, she went to bed a couple of hours ago. She hasn't slept much in the past twenty-four hours," Barb answered.

"Yeah," Cass said. She tensed when she felt Barb's grip on her knee tighten.

"Tell me what happened."

"Nothing happened," Cass said, but even as the words left her mouth she knew it wasn't true. And Barb knew it too if the look on her face was any indication.

Cass hung her head in defeat. She knew from past experiences Barb would stay silent until Cass told her everything, so she did. Starting with the night before when she and Erica had gone to her cabin, and ending with the kiss on her way out the door that evening. She intentionally left out the earlier talk with her mother though. When she was done, she finally looked up to see Barb watching her intently.

Barb sat back and crossed her arms over her chest but never broke their eye contact. Cass fought to not squirm under her gaze.

"Are you going to say something soon? I could really use a drink," Cass said after a few minutes had passed. Barb waved a hand to dismiss her, and Cass went to the kitchen to pour herself a shot of whiskey. She returned to the living room with a bottle of beer and reclaimed her seat a few beats before Barb broke her silence.

"Why do you insist on keeping women at arm's length?"

"What?" The question caught Cass off guard, and she didn't know what to say.

"You never bring anyone here to meet us, and you never talk about any one woman in particular. You always talk about women in the abstract."

"You know why."

"I know the reasons you've told me, but it's pretty obvious Erica's different." Barb moved forward again to rest her elbows on her knees. "She's gotten into your head, Cass, and I don't understand why you're fighting it so hard. Not to mention you're giving her mixed signals."

Cass swallowed hard and looked at the bottle she held in her hands. Barb was right. The mixed signals had to stop. No more going to her house and having make-out sessions on the couch, or at the front door. It was time to move on.

"No," Barb said. When Cass looked up she saw Barb shaking her head emphatically. "No. I can see the wheels spinning in your head, and you're wrong. Whatever it is you're thinking, you need to do the exact opposite. Trust me."

"How the fuck do you do that?"

"Watch your language. There are little ears in the house now, and I will not have you or your brother teaching him how to talk like a sailor before he even says Mama. Understood?" Barb waited until Cass nodded to continue. "You are not destined to repeat the mistakes of your mother, Cass. I know you're worried and think you'll get trapped in a relationship with a woman who wants to control you. Who wants you to give up your dream and demand you get a real job. Honestly, Erica doesn't strike me as the type to do those things."

"You may very well be right," Cass said. Hell, she'd even caught herself thinking the same thing more than once since the night before. But after tonight, the stakes had risen. "She's going to try to gain guardianship of her brother."

"Kyle seems like a good kid."

"He is, but don't you see? It wouldn't just be me and her. We're talking about a ready-made family here, Barb." Cass felt her heart speed up at the mere thought of it. "Some months I can't even afford to buy enough food for me and Gordy, let alone two other people."

"Are you really this dense?" Barb looked at her and Cass could tell she was trying really hard not to laugh. Cass didn't see anything funny in the situation. "Do you like her?"

"You know I do."

"Okay, and you like Kyle?"

"Of course." Cass wondered what the hell any of this had to do with anything at all, and she let her frustration show when she set the beer bottle down harder than necessary and ran both hands through her hair.

"She works for the post office, Cass. The federal government. Do you have any idea how much money those people make? I highly doubt she would ever count on someone else to take care of her financially."

"So she'd end up supporting me and then I'd be indebted to her. That's an even better scenario, isn't it?" Cass asked. She clapped her hands together once and stood to leave. This conversation wasn't helping.

"Really? You think Danny feels that way because I'm a doctor with a steady income?"

"Not what I meant. At all."

"Of course it is. There's not much else you could have meant with that comment."

"Tell me you aren't pushing him to get a job now since there's another mouth to feed."

"What?" Barb looked truly shocked by her words. "He's doing what he loves. He's doing what makes him happy. If I asked him to make such a drastic change in his life, he wouldn't be the man I fell in love with. And besides, most of the time you guys are here all day, so I don't have to worry about leaving Clarence with a babysitter so often."

Cass was lucky she was still close enough to the chair so she could sit again, because her knees almost gave out.

"So you're content to let him keep doing storage auctions?"

"Absolutely. Has he told you differently?"

"I just assumed," Cass said. She felt like an idiot. How could she not have seen the differences in the dynamics of her parents' relationship compared to Danny and Barb's? Maybe her mother had been right, and it was possible to have it all.

Barb certainly made a good argument for why she should pursue something with Erica, but deep down, Cass knew it would never work. She'd always be waiting for it to end, and therefore wouldn't be able to truly enjoy their time together. She found herself wondering when exactly she stopped worrying so much about Erica controlling her life, and began worrying she wouldn't be able to keep Erica happy. She closed her eyes against the pain starting in the back of her head.

"You should know better than to assume," Barb told her as she stood. "Just promise me you'll think about the things I said. Don't write Erica off because you don't think you can make her happy."

"I promise." Cass got to her feet and allowed Barb to give her a hug and a kiss on the cheek.

"Good. I'm going to bed now. Just make sure you lock the door on your way out."

Cass did as she asked and made her way down the path to her cabin. There was no way she could keep the promise she'd made though. Cass knew, deep down inside, she could never make Erica happy for long. It was better for them both to just leave things where they stood. Cass would be a much better friend than a wife.

CHAPTER TWENTY

It was a week later when Barb insisted on them all going out to dinner. Cass didn't want to go. She still hadn't talked to Erica since the night she'd run out on her, and she was feeling a bit ill-tempered. She'd tried to beg off, but between Barb, Danny, and her mother, she didn't stand a chance. And then there was Clarence—or Rance, as they'd started calling him, thank God. He had the bluest eyes, and the cutest smile. Cass didn't think she'd be able to refuse him anything.

"I want to go on record as saying I think this is a bad idea," Cass said from the backseat of her mother's rental car. Danny was up front, and Barb was in back with her, Rance securely situated in his car seat between them.

"Your protest is duly noted, dear, but I do hope you'll at least try to enjoy yourself," her mother said. Cass caught her eye in the rearview mirror and her mother winked at her.

"I don't know why you couldn't have just let me stay home." Cass crossed her arms over her chest and turned her head to watch the fields go by. Spring had finally arrived in western New York, and the snow was melting away. Soon these fields would be teeming with migrant workers planting the crops for a new season.

"I don't know why you can't just pick up the phone and call her," Barb said. When Cass whipped her head around to glare at her, Barb simply shrugged. "You know you want to."

"What makes you think you know what I want?"

"Tell me I'm wrong, and I'll let it go."

The silence in the car was deafening. Cass noticed Danny had turned in his seat to look at her, and her mother's eyes kept darting back and forth between the road and the rearview mirror. They were all waiting for her to either admit or deny her desire to call Erica. She looked down at the baby, as if she thought he might be able to get her out of this mess. He smiled at her. Or, more likely, it was merely gas.

"I thought we talked about this, Cass," her mother finally said.

"We did, and it was a private conversation, wasn't it?" Cass hoped her tone made it clear it was to stay between the two of them. She didn't need Danny and Barb privy to what they'd discussed.

"Fine."

They were all silent on the remainder of the trip to Batavia. Cass was out of the car first, desperately in need of some fresh air. She hoped it might clear her head and help her to find a better state of mind. She lagged behind the rest of them as they walked into Applebee's and waited for the hostess to seat them. A quick glance into the bar area and she felt as though she'd been punched in the gut. Erica was there. With a woman.

Barb, ever intuitive, followed her line of sight and gasped just before placing a hand on Cass's arm. Cass shook her head and forced herself to look away. What did she care? She wasn't seeing Erica, and had made the fact abundantly clear the last time they'd parted ways. But if that were the case, then why did she have a gnawing feeling in the pit of her stomach?

"Hey, you okay?" Barb asked quietly.

"Fine." Cass was grateful Barb didn't draw attention to the fact she'd been blindsided. She forced a smile. "I'm fine."

Barb didn't look convinced. Cass felt helpless to stop herself from stealing another glance at Erica and her date. They were laughing, and Cass flinched when she saw Erica put a hand on the other woman's leg, suggesting they were more than just friends.

"Cass, come on," Danny said.

She returned her attention to her family and saw they were being led into the dining area. She concentrated hard on walking without tripping over anything, especially her own feet. Barb slowed until Cass caught up with her.

"The woman's too old for her, you know. It can't be anything serious."

"It doesn't matter," Cass said, trying to sound unaffected by what she'd seen. She wasn't sure she was pulling it off, based on Barb's expression. "I told her we could be friends. It's good she's moving on."

"Wow," Barb said, shaking her head. "You are one cold bitch, aren't you?"

"Let it go," Cass told her.

"What's going on?" her mother asked when they were all seated.

"Erica's in the bar with another woman," Barb said.

Cass fought the urge to kick her under the table. Instead, she picked up her menu and pretended to be reading it. In reality, she couldn't make sense of a single word.

"Would you mind leaving us for a few moments?" her mother asked them.

Cass lowered the menu to look at her mother even as Barb and Danny stood. When Barb started to pick up the baby carrier, her mother spoke again.

"Leave him. Just for a few moments."

When they were gone, Cass folded her menu and sat back in her seat. She was happy she was sitting where she was and had no view of the bar, because she knew she wouldn't have the willpower to keep from watching Erica with her date.

"You told me things went well between the two of you the other night."

"I lied."

"Cassidy. What happened?"

"I can't change everything about myself based on a single conversation," Cass told her. "I've lived so long avoiding any kind of commitment, I'm afraid it's just who I am now."

"But why lie to me about it?"

Cass's shoulders sagged when she saw the undeniable disappointment in her mother's eyes. She'd never lied to her before, and she felt bad about it.

"So you'd leave me alone about it," she answered, knowing it was a feeble excuse, but at a complete loss at any other explanation. "Between you, Barb, and Danny, I don't feel like I'm in control of my life anymore."

"And Erica?"

She was right, and Cass knew it. Erica had everything to do with her not feeling in control of *anything*. She'd never felt this way before, and she didn't like it. The stab of jealousy was like a knife through her heart. It was a foreign feeling for her, yet she recognized it immediately. *She* should be the one sitting in the bar with Erica, making her laugh, feeling the touch of her hand on her thigh.

"Oh, Cass," her mother said as she slid into the booth next to her. Cass didn't fight it when she put her arms around her. She let her mother hold her, but she refused to cry. She was vaguely aware of the server asking if everything was all right, and her mother assuring her they were fine. "Sweetheart, you need to talk to her. Tell her how you feel, and why you're so afraid."

"It's too late for that," Cass said as she pulled away from her. She ran a hand through her hair and blew out a frustrated breath. "She's here with someone else, and I just need to accept it. I'll be fine."

Her mother looked skeptical, and her expression summed up exactly how Cass felt. She pulled herself together just as she saw Danny and Barb heading back toward the table, their waitress following close behind with a tray full of drinks from the bar. Cass smiled at them. Maybe getting drunk would take the pain of jealousy away.

❖

"Dear, what is it? You look like you've seen a ghost."

Erica was staring at Barb and Danny as they walked out of the bar and into the main restaurant. She considered going after them, but she felt rooted to her seat. Her aunt's voice managed to pull her back

"I'm sorry, what?"

"You look upset, Erica. What's going on?"

"I thought I saw her earlier, but I was sure I must have imagined it," Erica said. She'd picked Applebee's for dinner because she knew Cass didn't care for it. She'd never dreamed she'd run into her here, of all places. "But now I know I did. Her brother and his wife were just at the bar."

"Cassidy?" Lila asked, craning her neck to look into the dining room as if she'd recognize Cass if she saw her. She finally turned back to Erica. "I want to meet the woman who's managed to turn your world upside down."

"She obviously doesn't want to see me, so I'd wager a meeting tonight isn't in the cards," Erica said with a wry smile. Lila, her father's sister, had come from Jamestown to visit for a few days, and Erica had been glad to see her. She'd just arrived that day and insisted they go out for dinner. Kyle couldn't join them because he had too much homework to get done since he'd missed more than a week of school.

"Then she's a fool who doesn't deserve someone like you." Lila smiled, and Erica thought, not for the first time since she'd rolled into town, how good Lila looked.

When she'd opened the door to find Lila on the porch, she hadn't recognized her at first. Plastic surgery reversed what Mother Nature had done to her over the years, and Lila appeared nearly twenty years younger.

"Thank you," Erica said. "I needed to hear that."

"It's true, and don't you let anyone tell you differently." Lila covered Erica's hand and waited until Erica met her gaze, "The way your parents treated you when you came out to them was unforgivable. I think a lot of people would have curled up in a corner and withered away, but you picked yourself up and made something of yourself. And what you're doing for Kyle, well, if this woman can't see what an amazing person you are, then it's her loss."

Erica nodded, unable to speak around the lump in her throat. She blinked a few times to fight back the tears she could feel threatening. Lila was the one who was amazing as far as Erica was concerned. It had been many years ago, but Lila had lost a husband and a son within months of each other, and her own brother had turned his back on her. How could two people who'd grown up together turn out so differently?

"What was unforgivable was how my father treated you after Barry committed suicide," Erica said, referring to Lila's son, her cousin.

"Don't you worry about that."

"But I do. I feel like someone needs to apologize for the things he said to you."

"You're right," Lila said after a few moments of obvious reflection. "But it shouldn't be you, sweetheart. I haven't spoken to your father since the day of Barry's funeral, and I don't expect I ever will again. *I'm* sorry for having convinced you to tell them you were gay. I thought if it was his own child he'd feel differently."

They were both silent then, and Erica couldn't help but think back to the day of her cousin's funeral. Erica had been fourteen, and Barry had only been three years older when he'd taken his own life. Erica remembered being shocked by the things her father said to Lila, but she'd never let him know she'd heard any of it.

It still made her cringe to think her father had told Lila she should consider herself lucky Barry took his own life. That way, she wouldn't have to watch him lead a life of sin and wither away to nothing after he contracted AIDS. Barry's funeral had been three months to the day after Lila's husband died of lung cancer.

Erica remembered doing a mental happy dance when Lila slapped her father hard enough to leave a mark lasting for days after.

Her father never did offer a plausible explanation as to why Lila moved away after the funeral and never called or came to visit. Erica had already known by fourteen she was a lesbian, but there was no way in hell she was going to tell her parents after what happened with Lila. Once she'd turned eighteen, she drove to Jamestown and reconnected with Lila. They'd been close ever since.

"You don't need to apologize," Erica said with a quick shake of her head. "I was the one who couldn't stomach lying to them any longer. Like you, I'd hoped they'd feel differently about it when it was their own. We were both wrong."

"I just wish Kyle would have waited until he was older to come out to them," Lila said.

"Me too, and I begged him to wait until he graduated, but he couldn't lie to them any longer either, and I can't say I blame him. He's growing up in a world where more and more people are accepting of the LGBT community. He thought maybe they'd evolved as well."

"Evolving isn't something the Jacobs men ever did easily," Lila said with a wry grin. "Your father came by his views and his stubbornness quite honestly."

Erica smiled and they finished their dinner in silence. When the waiter picked up the bill from their table, she stood and put her coat on. They headed for the door, but Lila stopped her just before she reached it.

"Are you sure you don't want to say something to her?"

Erica thought about it for a moment before shaking her head and walking out to the car. Of course she wanted to say something. The past week had been hell wondering every day if Cass would come in to the post office to mail some packages. But it was Danny who was coming in every day instead.

She was done trying to convince Cass she'd be okay with a casual arrangement. If Cass was interested, she could initiate a conversation.

CHAPTER TWENTY-ONE

Two more weeks passed, and Cass continued to avoid seeing Erica at the post office. Of course, it helped that Danny agreed to ship almost everything during those weeks, but Cass saw it as a victory. She'd only wanted to call Erica every day, but she'd somehow managed to refrain. On the other hand, so had Erica, a fact that stung more than she was willing to acknowledge. Danny wasn't stupid, and Cass was sure he knew what was going on. How many times could something come up so she couldn't make it to the post office?

"Let me guess," he said as he leaned against the doorframe of the garage with a knowing smile. "You suddenly need to give Gordy a bath, so you need me to go to the post office."

Cass wanted to slap the smile right off his face. She'd never wanted anything so much in her life. Unless you counted Erica, which she refused to do. She glanced down at Gordy, who was sleeping by the packages she'd gotten ready to ship out. "He is pretty dirty."

"I'm an enabler." Danny took a couple of steps toward her. "You know that, right?"

"That's an awfully big word for someone with a pea brain. Are you just repeating what Barb tells you again?"

"Very funny."

"An enabler is usually a bad thing, isn't it? If I were an alcoholic and you covered for me when I got drunk, or bought me liquor, you'd be an enabler."

"Barb says you denying your feelings for Erica is a bad thing, and my going to the post office every day is enabling you to continue denying it."

"See? I knew she's the one who put the idea in your head." Cass turned her back on him to finish up the last package. The sooner she was done, the sooner she could go home and veg out for the rest of the night.

"I can't go to the auctions with you tomorrow." Danny threw it out there like it was no big deal. But it was to Cass. He started to reach for the packages, but she grabbed his arm.

"Why not?" she asked, trying not to let her temper get the best of her. "There's like fifty units tomorrow. You'll be able to help me do the cleanouts on Saturday, right?"

"I don't know." Danny shrugged and looked apologetic, but Cass sensed something else was going on. Something she wasn't going to like. "I have to take Rance to the doctor tomorrow. He's got a bit of a fever, and Barb just wants to be safe. She has to work on Saturday, so if somebody needs to stay with him, I won't be able to help you."

Cass let out a laugh, but there was no humor in it, and Danny knew it. He took a step back, expecting her to blow up, no doubt. She knew what Barb was doing, and she didn't believe for a second Rance had a fever at all. They were playing her. Their mother was still in town and was more than capable of looking after a sick baby. They were just trying to force her to call Erica so she could ask Kyle to help her on Saturday. She shook her head as she went back to putting the shipping label on the box she was working on.

"Ask Erica if Kyle's available to help me then."

"Cass—"

"Ask her, damn it," she said. "If you really aren't able to help me, then it's up to you to find someone to be there in your place."

She shoved the box into his midsection and whistled for Gordy to follow her. She didn't give a rat's ass what he and Barb thought. Cass would clear out the units herself before she'd call Erica and ask for her help.

She slammed the front door and headed straight for the kitchen. Beer in hand, she collapsed onto the sofa and stared at the ceiling. One o'clock on a Thursday afternoon, and she was drinking already. Oh well, it had to be five o'clock somewhere, right?

Gordy jumped up next to her and rested his head in her lap. She absently ruffled his fur and he sighed his contentment. He licked the hand clutching the beer bottle and she looked down at him. It dawned on her the only time in the past three weeks she'd not been completely on edge was when she sat here with Gordy. It had to stop.

She hadn't been sleeping much, and when she did drift off, she'd only wake up a few minutes later after dreaming about Erica. She'd been ill-tempered toward Danny, Barb, and her mother, but it was almost as if she couldn't help herself. Anything they said to her seemed to rub her the wrong way, and if they mentioned Erica, forget about it.

How the hell had Erica gotten so completely under her skin in such a short period of time? No one had ever been able to make her think twice about them, and there'd been plenty of women who'd tried. Gordy lifted his head and gave her chin a quick swipe of his tongue. She kissed him on the snout and rubbed behind his ear.

"Maybe I just need to get laid," she said to the ceiling. Maybe it could be that simple, but she had no desire to drive to Buffalo or Rochester, and there sure as hell wasn't anywhere local the lesbians hung out at. In fact, there were people who would deny right to her face that any lesbians lived in this town. She chuckled before taking a swig of her beer. It was mindboggling how people were able to only see what they chose to see. She could tell someone she was a lesbian, and they'd insist she was wrong. "Because there aren't any of *those people* around here."

Gordy chuffed and rubbed his nose against her leg as if he were laughing at what she'd said. God, she really did need to get out more. If she thought the dog was communicating with her, how far behind could crazy town be?

She jumped when there was a loud banging at the door. She pushed Gordy off the couch when he started barking and ran to the kitchen to put her beer back in the fridge. After shoving a piece of spearmint gum in her mouth, she hurried to answer the door.

"I'm leaving now," Danny told her. "You're going to keep an eye on Rance for me, right?"

"Absolutely," she said with a smile. She grabbed her coat and followed him up the path. "But you'll only be gone for a few minutes, and he never wakes up while you're gone."

"But if he did, someone needs to be there, not to mention the fact Barb would kill me if she found out I left him alone for any longer than it took me to walk to your place and back."

"And you wonder why I'm not interested in a long-term relationship," she mumbled. She ran right into his back when he stopped abruptly. She took a step back and he turned to face her, looking more pissed off than she'd ever seen him before.

"You do know it's just a figure of speech, right? She wouldn't really kill me."

"Yeah, I know, but it really isn't the point."

"Then what is, Cass? I've tried to be the laid-back little brother, but I can't deal with you like this anymore. You've been itching for a fight for three weeks now. I'm at the end of my rope with you, so tell me, Cassidy, what is the point?"

She stared at him. She knew her mouth was hanging open, but she couldn't help it. He'd never pushed her back like this, and she didn't know how to deal with it. Part of her felt bad for having backed him far enough into a corner to make him fight back, but she wasn't herself lately. Everything she did felt wrong, and she didn't know why. And now Danny was accusing her of trying to pick a fight. If that was what he wanted, she'd give it to him.

"You're tied down. You can't do anything without your wife's permission, Daniel. That's my point. I don't want any part of it."

"Because I can't go with you tomorrow?" he asked, his tone full of incredulity. "The world doesn't revolve around you, Cass, and it's about time you realized it. Yes, I do things she tells me to do, and she does things I tell her to do. It's a partnership, and we work together. We are not like Mom and Dad, and if you'd pull your head out of your ass long enough to look at the world around you, you'd see most marriages aren't like theirs."

Cass pushed past him and continued up the path to the house. Her pulse was pounding so loudly in her ears she didn't hear him stomping up behind her. She almost lost her footing when he grabbed her by the arm and forced her to turn around.

"Get your hands off me unless you want to end up in the hospital," she said through clenched teeth. He let go and backed away, obviously sensing she meant what she was saying. She wouldn't have hurt him, at least she didn't think she would, but she felt like what she imagined a cornered dog might feel like, and her instinct was to fight. "Go to the damn post office so I can get on with my evening."

It was his turn to push past her, but as soon as he was far enough away, he sent one last verbal jab at her.

"I sure as hell hope your evening plans include getting laid, because I've about had enough of this shit for one lifetime."

Chapter Twenty-two

Erica was almost done with her shift when she saw Danny walking into the lobby. She waved him over, and he began tossing packages on the counter from the hand truck he'd used to haul them in from the car.

"How are you today?" she asked as she began weighing them to make sure they carried the correct postage. She felt as if she was wasting her time, because he'd never been wrong yet, but it was procedure.

"Shitty, if you want to know the truth."

Erica just looked at him, not knowing how to respond. After a moment, he waved a hand in the air between them and smiled. It didn't look genuine to her, but she wasn't about to say anything about it.

"Cass and I had a fight."

Erica nodded slowly, still not quite sure what to say. He didn't seem to notice her lack of participation in the conversation though.

"We came this close," he said, holding his thumb and forefinger mere millimeters apart, "to using our fists. Well, she did, anyway. I would never hit a woman, no matter what."

"Good to know," Erica said.

"I'm sorry. You don't need to listen to me bitch about my sister." Danny leaned on the counter and let out a breath before pasting the obviously fake smile on his face again. "How are you doing?"

"Fine."

It was a lie, but she wasn't about to tell him she missed Cass. Missed having her come in to ship packages, missed having her come by the house. And she sure as hell wasn't going to tell him how much she missed kissing her. Nope, not going there.

"Cass misses you." Danny looked surprised at his own words, and Erica tried not to laugh when he looked around to see if anybody else was in earshot.

"I doubt it," Erica said with a slow shake of her head.

"She does," he said, and for some reason she believed him. Or maybe she just desperately wanted it to be true, so it was easier to believe him than not. "She's miserable. She's trying to pick a fight with me anytime I say something to her."

"And what would make you think it has anything to do with me?"

"She took the game console to Kyle one night, and I'm pretty sure you two haven't spoken to each other since. Am I right?" He waited until she finally nodded her response before continuing. "I've never seen her like this. I mean, like, *ever*. And she comes up with the lamest excuses for not being able to come here to ship packages."

"She knows I get off at two thirty. All she'd have to do is come in after I'm gone if she wants to avoid seeing me so much. Or she could always go to a different office." Erica realized she was handling the packages a little too roughly and took a deep breath in an attempt to center herself.

"Why would she want to avoid you?" Danny asked, and her finger stopped on its way to the keyboard so she could print out his receipt so he'd have proof the boxes were actually shipped. "I mean, just think about it for a second. What possible reason could she have to avoid you?"

Erica handed him the receipt and placed her hands on the counter in front of her. She felt something deep down inside she hadn't experienced in far too long. Hope. But no, Danny had to be wrong. He obviously didn't know how they'd ended things the night in question. Cass must have lied to him and told him everything had gone swimmingly. Otherwise he wouldn't be asking her that question. Erica wasn't going to push Cass to see her again based on Danny's observations, because she'd always hated needy people, and she refused to become one. She looked up at him, not knowing quite what to say, and his next words caught her off guard.

"Is Kyle free on Saturday?"

"As far as I know, why?"

"I have to stay home with the baby, so I can't help Cass clean out the units she's probably going to buy at auction tomorrow."

"Why doesn't she just call and ask?"

"Apparently, since I'm the one who's not showing up for work, it's my job to find someone to take my place."

Erica nodded again and took the packages to the back as she tried to form a response in her head. She wasn't sure she could manage it without being snarky. It hurt that Cass hadn't bothered to call over the past few weeks, and she tried not to let anyone see it bothered her to have Danny shipping their packages every day. Did he really think she hadn't noticed? Why *was* Cass trying so hard to avoid her? They'd agreed to be friends, so why was there so much distance between them now? When she returned to the counter, Danny was still there, obviously waiting for her response. It was time to put an end to this.

"Tell her if she wants Kyle's help, she'll have to call me and talk about it."

Danny's smile was genuine now, and he looked like a man who'd had a huge weight lifted off his shoulders. He clasped her hand and brought it to his lips for a quick kiss.

"Thank you," he said. He squeezed her hand before he let go. "You have no idea how much I wanted to hear those words. I think I probably would have told her that even if you hadn't said it, but this makes it so much better. Thank you."

Erica watched, dumbfounded, as he turned and practically ran out of the building. She heard a noise behind her and turned to see Trish approaching from the back.

"What was all that about?"

"Cassidy Holmes," Erica answered.

"Really?" Trish looked surprised. "Are you two serious?"

"No," Erica forced a laugh and shook her head. "We're just friends."

"Sure you are. Then why would her brother be kissing your hand and falling all over himself thanking you for wanting her to call you?"

"How long were you listening?"

"Long enough."

"We're just friends," Erica said again. "Unfortunately."

"We're going to have to go for a drink some night so you can tell me all about it." Trish laughed when Erica gave her a shocked look. "What? My husband spends way too much time on the road. I need to live vicariously through others. And right now, that means you."

❖

Erica kept looking at her cell phone all evening, wondering if Cass had called and she'd somehow missed it. After what seemed like the fiftieth time, Kyle looked at her in frustration.

"What the hell is wrong with you tonight?"

"Nothing," she said, shaking her head and trying to concentrate on the television show they were watching. She hadn't wanted to like *The Walking Dead,* but Kyle managed to talk her into watching the first couple of episodes on Netflix. *Binge watching*, he'd called it. She had to admit it sucked her in, and now she was probably more into it than he was.

"Bull," he said. "Why do you keep looking at your phone?"

"What are you doing on Saturday?"

"Nothing." He pressed the pause button on the remote and turned in his seat to face her. "Why? Does this have to do with Mom and Dad?"

"What? No," she said. "God, no."

"And it has nothing to do with you and the guardianship thing?"

"No, it's got absolutely nothing to do with that." She looked at her phone again and then slammed it against her leg, cursing herself for waiting to get a call she knew probably wasn't coming. "Cass might need your help cleaning out some storage units."

"Cool. Does this mean you two are talking again?"

"Not exactly." She shook her head. "Danny was in today to ship some packages and he mentioned it. I told him to have her call me."

"Why aren't you talking? You never told me what happened." Kyle watched her, an expectant look on his face. "I mean, one minute you're on the couch kissing, and the next you aren't even talking to her."

"I did tell you, Kyle. We want different things out of life."

"Yeah, I know, and I get it, but you said you were going to be friends, but now obviously you aren't. I feel a little strange helping her when you guys aren't even talking."

"Don't feel strange, Kyle, all right? She helped you when you needed it, and she's a good person. Don't feel guilty for helping her. She and I will work things out, okay?" Erica wasn't sure she believed what she was saying, so how could she expect Kyle to?

Much to her surprise, he seemed to take what she said for the truth because he nodded and turned back to the TV as he pushed the button to start the show again. Erica sighed in defeat when she looked one last time at her phone. She tossed it onto the table and settled in to watch some zombies get killed. A few seconds later, the phone rang, and Erica instantly felt as though the air was sucked out of the room. She grabbed for it, but the letdown she experienced at seeing the name *Lila* instead of the name she was hoping for was palpable. Kyle paused the show again as she stood and walked into the kitchen.

"Hi, Lila," she said, trying to inject some of her usual cheerfulness into her voice.

"Hey, sweetie," came the reply.

"It's good to hear your voice," Erica said after a moment.

"Yours too. Have you talked to Cassidy yet?"

"No." Erica fought against the lump forming in her throat. She glanced over her shoulder at Kyle, who was visibly trying to listen without being obvious. She smiled but decided he didn't need to hear her talking about Cass. "We're doing pretty well. Thank you though. I've enrolled Kyle in school here, and I'm working on gaining guardianship."

She went into her bedroom and they talked for the next hour, and Erica told her everything she was feeling about Cass. Erica went to bed feeling a little more optimistic than she had earlier in the evening. True, Cass hadn't called, but at least she had someone to talk to about it.

Chapter Twenty-three

Cass cursed under her breath as she put a lock on her third unit of the day. She'd promised herself she wouldn't bid on anything that looked like it would be too much for her to move on her own. And now, here she was with three units, and every one of them full of furniture. She looked at her watch and saw it was only noon. She was going to have to call Erica sometime and ask if Kyle would be able to help her the next day.

She'd been pissed when Danny came home the previous day and told her what Erica had said. She'd spent the evening drinking and watching *The Walking Dead* on DVD for the umpteenth time, but never once thought about picking up the phone. No, that wasn't entirely true, she reminded herself. After her fifth beer, she'd started to call Erica, but reason prevailed when she realized drunk dialing was never a good idea.

She was paying for those beers today. She blamed the hangover for her lapse of judgment in the units she was bidding on. Maybe deep down she wanted to have to call Erica, but on the surface, she balked at the idea. It was childish, she knew, to be avoiding her at all costs, but Erica certainly could have made the effort to get in touch with her too.

"Flying solo again?"

Cass turned to see Rodney behind her, and she grimaced outwardly. She hadn't seen him since she'd been rude to him, and while she still felt bad about it, she no longer cared. If he was going to be an ass to her today, he was going to bite off more than he could chew. It wasn't like this facility to allow latecomers access to the auction, but she supposed he knew someone who worked there.

"I'm not in the mood today."

"And that's different than normal how?"

"Look, I'm not—"

"Chill out, Holmes, Jesus," he said. "I'm not here to bother you. I just wanted to say hello and to let you know there are no hard feelings, all right?"

Cass nodded once before turning away and going to join the bidders at the next unit. She knew she should apologize for lashing out, but damn it, she couldn't help it. It seemed as if everyone in the entire universe was getting on her last nerve.

There was nothing else worth bidding on, so she let all the gawkers fight over the remaining units. When they were done, Cass walked to her truck and pulled her phone out of her pocket, dreading the call she was being forced to make. Her palms were actually sweating, in spite of the chilly temperature, and her pulse was pounding. It was after three now, so she knew Erica would be done with work, but she hesitated in hitting the call button.

She slammed the door of the truck closed so she could enjoy what little heat the sun was providing in the cab and tried to think things out rationally. They had agreed to be friends, right? Then why hadn't Erica bothered to call? Erica was probably wondering the same thing about her, but Cass shook her head. She couldn't allow those thoughts to muddy her mind any more than it already was.

She pushed the call button before she could talk herself out of it again, and held her breath waiting to see if Erica would answer, or if she would ignore the call and let it go to voicemail. On the fourth ring, Cass was about to disconnect when she heard Erica's voice.

"Cass?" she said, sounding like she was out of breath.

"Hey, are you busy?" Cass asked. It was strange, but just hearing Erica's voice seemed to center her. She felt calmer than she had in what seemed like years.

"No, I was just cleaning out Willie's litter box," she said, then chuckled. "Sorry. I guess you didn't need to know that."

"Probably not," Cass answered, smiling to herself as she felt her pulse slow. This was starting out well. At least Erica wasn't being pissy with her.

"So, did you need something?"

"I don't want to be *that* friend. You know, the one who only calls when they need something from you." Cass winced inwardly, because it was exactly why she was calling.

"Then you don't need something?" She sounded skeptical.

"Well, I do, but you already know that, don't you? Danny said he mentioned I might need Kyle's help tomorrow."

"He did. I sort of expected a call about it last night though."

Now she sounded a little pissy. Cass scrambled to think of something—anything—to say that wouldn't sound like she was making excuses, because, of course, she was.

"I figured there was no point in asking until I knew for sure I was going to need him." Silence came from the other end of the line, and Cass wasn't comfortable with it. She tapped her thumb nervously against the steering wheel, but she'd never been good with awkward quietness. "So, would it be all right with you if he helped me tomorrow?"

"It's okay with me, but I'd have to ask him if he's free. It is Saturday after all, and he might have other plans I don't know about."

Cass wondered if this was Erica's way of brushing her off. She didn't believe for a second Erica wouldn't be aware of what plans Kyle may have made for the weekend. She took in a deep breath and glanced out the side window. The line of people paying for the units they'd purchased was dwindling faster than she'd expected.

"All right. Should I call him later, after you've had a chance to ask him about it, or do you want to have him call me?" Cass asked as she raked a hand through her hair. She had to get inside and pay before the auctioneer packed up his things and left.

"I'll have him call you later tonight," Erica answered. She sounded like she wanted to say more, and Cass wanted to hear it, but not now.

"Cool," she said as she hopped out of the truck and began walking toward the building. "I'm sorry, but I have to go. I need to pay for the units I bought."

"Oh. Okay."

Cass experienced what felt strangely like a knife piercing her heart at the disappointment she heard in Erica's voice. Her step faltered as she managed to stop herself from asking Erica to have dinner with her. She couldn't do that. When she was with Erica, she forgot all about why it was a bad idea to want more than she'd ever wanted from anyone before. It would only lead to mixed signals, and Erica thinking there could actually be more than friendship between them. At this point though, Cass was beginning to understand being friends might not even be possible.

"I'll talk to you later, all right?" Cass asked, her voice softening.

"Sure." Erica ended the call then, not even bothering to say good-bye.

Cass stopped walking and stared at the phone, wondering when everything had begun to go so horribly wrong between them.

Chapter Twenty-four

"You have no idea how much I appreciate you helping me out today," Cass said as she pulled the padlock of the first unit and raised the door.

"You've said that already," Kyle told her. She looked at him and saw he was smiling.

"I did?"

"Yeah. More than once, actually." He took a step back when he saw how packed the unit was. "Damn. You sure we'll be able to clean out all of this today?"

"That's the goal," she said with a shrug. "Although I do have until the end of business Monday to get it done."

"In other words you're going to work me like a dog today."

"Pretty much, yeah." Cass laughed at the look on his face. She clapped him on the shoulder. "Relax, Kyle. I'll buy you lunch *and* dinner in exchange for your help."

"McDonald's or Burger King?" His tone was indicative of his distaste for fast food, which Cass found rather strange in a teenager. She thought they all lived for their next burger fix.

"How about Arby's for lunch, and maybe I'll take you somewhere nicer for dinner, if you work all day without complaining, deal?"

"You might regret that," he said with a grin. "I'm still growing. You have no idea how much I can actually eat."

"Sounds like we might be going to an all you can eat buffet then."

They worked until one in the afternoon and almost had the first unit completely cleaned out. Unfortunately, no matter how they moved things around, it didn't look like there'd be enough room to fit much else in the truck. By the time they had lunch and took the truck home to unload it all, there wouldn't be a whole lot of daylight left.

"You up for doing this again tomorrow?" she asked him when they sat down in Arby's with their lunch. She unwrapped her sandwich and took a big bite, not realizing just how hungry she'd been until then.

"As long as it's all right with my sister," he answered with a shrug.

At his words, it occurred to Cass she would have to see Erica when she dropped him off at home. Erica was already at work when she'd picked him up that morning, so she hadn't been forced into an uncomfortable situation. She had a feeling her luck in avoiding Erica was about to run out. Maybe if she took Kyle out for dinner, Erica might be in bed by the time she dropped him off because she was at work now. Which meant she'd gotten up at four in the morning.

"After we eat we'll take this load back and empty the truck. Any ideas where you might like to eat dinner?"

"You don't have to feed me tonight," he told her.

"I said I would. It's not a problem. You've been a huge help today, and hopefully tomorrow too. It's the least I can do."

"Well, when you put it that way…" He put his burger down and looked at her as he wiped his hands on a napkin. "Would you mind if Erica joined us for dinner? I know she doesn't have plans, and I'm pretty sure she'd like to see you."

Cass looked down at her curly fries and refused to meet his eyes. What had Erica told him about why they hadn't seen each other in over three weeks? They'd managed to not talk about her and Erica all morning, and she'd begun to hope the trend would last all day. Would it be rude to deny his request? She knew it would be. He cleared his throat and she looked at him, her appetite gone when she saw his hopeful expression.

"Of course. Go ahead and call her later." Cass took a drink of her soda and knew she wouldn't be finishing her lunch. Her stomach was in knots in anticipation of seeing Erica again. "We can pick her up if she's interested in joining us."

"She will be."

Cass nodded and smiled, wondering at the butterflies in her midsection. It was a totally new feeling, and she wasn't sure what to make of it. The last time she'd experienced anything even remotely similar was the first time she'd kissed another girl.

❖

"You two looked like you could use a break."

Cass turned at the sound of her mother's voice and smiled at her. She could definitely use a break, and she knew Kyle could too, but she had the feeling he wouldn't admit it under normal circumstances. They were almost done unloading, just a couch and a couple of dressers to go. But it could wait for a few minutes. She took the bottles of water her mother held out to her and tossed one of them to Kyle.

"Mom, this is Kyle Jacobs," she said before taking a long drink. "Kyle, my mother."

"It's nice to meet you, Cass's mother." Kyle grinned as he offered his hand to her.

Cass shook her head and smiled when her mother winked at her and grasped his hand. He was a charmer, of that there was no doubt.

"Please call me Sara," she told him before turning her attention to Cass. "Erica's brother, right?"

"You know Erica?" Kyle asked.

"No, I haven't yet had the pleasure, but I've heard an awful lot about her."

Cass felt like she should just finish unloading the truck herself. Apparently, these two were getting along just fine pretending she wasn't standing right there with them.

"Well, Cass is taking me out to dinner tonight as a way of thanking me for helping with all of this, and Erica is going to be joining us. Perhaps you'd like to come along too?"

Cass nearly choked on the water she was drinking, but instead she just snorted and it came out through her nose. Once she was done coughing and felt as though she could breathe normally again, she gave Kyle a look she hoped would make him shut up. The last thing she needed was for her mother to join them as well as Erica.

"Thank you so much for inviting me, Kyle, but I've already promised to make dinner for Danny and Barb this evening." She looked at Cass and smiled sweetly. "Maybe next time."

"She seems really nice," Kyle said when her mother was safely back in the house. He turned and went back into the truck.

This is just fan-freaking-tastic, Cass thought to herself. Now in addition to Barb and her mother, it appeared she had Kyle trying to be a matchmaker too.

❖

Erica was filling Willie's bowl with food when the front door opened and she heard Kyle and Cass laughing about something. She smiled as she stood up and walked into the living room. She stopped short when her eyes met Cass's and she couldn't look away.

"I'm going to take a quick shower," Kyle said, casting a glance at Cass and then Erica. He turned and left the room when it became apparent neither of them was going to answer.

"Hi," Cass said before looking away from her.

"Hi," Erica replied. Her heart sank as a realization hit her. She'd suspected it when Kyle called earlier and invited her to dinner. If Cass had wanted her to go with them, she would have called herself. "This wasn't your idea, was it?"

"No."

"I can stay here." Erica tried to hide her disappointment by sounding more cheerful than she thought she could. Cass looked at her, and Erica shrugged as if the whole situation wasn't tearing her apart. "I don't need to go."

"It's not that I don't want you to," Cass said, but then she looked away again and cleared her throat.

"But?"

"Damn it, Erica," Cass said.

They both glanced down the hall when they heard the water in the shower come on. Cass took a step or two closer to her, and she could see the hunger in Cass's eyes. Or was it anger? Erica couldn't really tell for sure, but she waited silently for Cass to continue, her heart beating a little faster than normal.

"I don't know how to act around you."

"Just be yourself."

"Really? Because I don't think I can be alone with you in a room and not think about ripping your clothes off. About moving my hands over your hips and under your ass. About you coming in my mouth, screaming out my name."

Erica sucked in a breath and gripped the counter next to her so she wouldn't fall over. Cass looked as though she wanted to come to her aid, but Erica shook her head and held a hand out to stop her. If Cass came anywhere near her now, she knew she'd drag her to the other end of the trailer and they'd both be naked in a matter of seconds. While the visual evoked from her words was hot as hell, Erica knew it wasn't the time or the place. And it probably never would be.

Cass looked surprised by her own words, and Erica watched, helpless, as Cass turned and reached for the door. She pulled it open and glanced back over her shoulder.

“I’m going to wait in the car,” she said before walking out. “I’m sorry.”

Erica managed to walk to the bath off the master bedroom and proceeded to splash cold water on her face. She stared at her reflection and wondered how she was going to manage to get through the evening. But she’d do it for Kyle. He didn’t know it, but while he was busy helping Cass again the next day, Erica was going to drive to Syracuse to make one last attempt at changing their parents’ minds about him, although she didn’t hold out much hope for it. And if reconciliation wasn’t possible, she had the papers from the lawyer for them to sign, giving up all parental rights to Kyle.

She figured he didn’t really need to know about it, and with any luck, she’d be back before they were. Lila had agreed to meet her there, for moral support. She knew from experience how difficult it could be to get through to Erica’s father.

Chapter Twenty-five

Cass wasn't feeling it. Dinner the night before had been strained, to say the least. Even Kyle threw his hands up in defeat and stopped trying to get them to talk to each other. And after being at the storage unit for over an hour, it appeared Kyle was fed up with the silence. They hadn't said anything since she picked him up.

"I've had enough," he said after depositing a heavy box in the truck and jumping down to meet her at eye level. She tried to go around him to get into the truck, but he moved to block her way up the ramp. "What the fuck is going on with you and Erica?"

"Are you supposed to talk like that?"

"Are you serious?" he asked, looking and sounding incredulous. He put his fists on his hips and stared her down. "You aren't my mother, or my sister, so you don't get to tell me how I can and can't talk. I couldn't get either of you to say a damn word to each other last night, but I thought I was going to combust from the heated looks between you. So tell me what's going on with you two."

"You wouldn't understand," Cass said. She tried once more to go around him, but he moved again. "You should ask her, because it isn't my place to talk to you about it."

"I wouldn't understand? Because I'm only sixteen?"

"You're fifteen," Cass reminded him.

"I'll be sixteen next week."

Kyle stood a little taller and she took a step back before putting down the box she was holding. It was obvious he wasn't going to let her continue working until they hashed this out.

"You'd best back down, Kyle," she said, trying to keep her anger in check. "You should remember we're in Buffalo. You want to start a fight? Because I could leave you here, and you'd have no way of getting home."

He sighed loudly and rolled his eyes as he crossed his arms over his chest and relaxed his stance. He stared at the ground and shook his head.

"Yeah, that's exactly what I want to do," he said after a moment. "Because fighting with a girl is something I've always dreamed of. You'll have to throw the first punch though, because I can only hit you if it's in self-defense."

"Fuck you," she said with a laugh. He joined her after a moment, and she felt a weight lifted off her shoulders. She sat on the end of the truck and motioned for him to join her. "I'm sorry. I know I shouldn't treat you like a kid, even though you technically are. I just think this is something you should talk to your sister about, all right?"

"I did. She said you don't want a relationship."

"I don't."

"I get that, sort of, but I can tell you guys like each other," he said, swinging his legs off the back of the truck. "Why can't you try?"

Cass thought for a moment, but couldn't come up with anything even remotely believable. It all sounded like pure crap, even in her own mind. She sighed when she realized it didn't really matter anyway, because Erica was seeing someone else now.

"Because failure scares the hell out of me," she finally said without looking at him. She knew she really shouldn't be talking to him about this, because he was a kid for God's sake.

"Failure scares me too, but do you think it stops me from playing football?"

"You play football." It was a statement rather than a question, and she knew she sounded more surprised than she should have. He was a decent sized guy, probably bigger than a lot of the kids playing high school sports, so why shouldn't he play? "I'm sorry, but I just don't picture you playing football. Baseball, yes. Maybe even basketball. But football? Really?"

"What? You think because I'm gay I can't like sports?"

Cass started to protest, but he laughed and punched her lightly on the arm.

"You're an ass, you know that?"

"So I've been told," he said, grinning. "All right, I don't play football, but my point is, if I did play, I wouldn't let the fear of failure hold me back."

"Things are different when you get older, Kyle. It isn't all black and white. You'll understand when you get to be my age."

"Jesus, you're ancient." He hopped down and headed back inside the unit, leaving Cass where she was. "It's gonna be forever until I reach your age."

"Enjoy your youth while you can," she called after him. She tilted her head back and gazed up at the sky. Spring made an appearance a couple of weeks earlier, pretty much melting all the snow on the ground. Mother Nature was evil sometimes though, and winter was trying to barrel its way back into western New York. The sky was gray, and it was starting to snow. Lightly, but it was still snow.

Cass was pulled out of her thoughts by a crash coming from inside the unit, and she heard Kyle cry out in what she assumed was pain. She ran inside quickly to find him pinned to the floor by a set of heavy metal shelves. She dropped to her knees and looked for any sign of blood around his head.

"Kyle, what happened?" she asked as she pulled her phone out to call for an ambulance. "Are you hurt? Did you hit your head?"

"Stop asking so many questions," he said before he winced. "Ow, shit, my leg is killing me."

Cass glanced down and saw a piece of metal protruding from his thigh. There was a lot of blood there, and she did her best to not let on what was wrong with the leg. She was no doctor, but it looked like it was probably broken too.

"Get these shelves off me," he cried when she was done on the phone.

"We've got to wait for the paramedics, all right? I don't want to risk hurting you more than you already are." Cass was doing a good job of remaining outwardly calm, but inside, her nerves were jangled. She thought she should keep him talking so he didn't go into shock. At least it was what they always did on those television shows. She decided it couldn't hurt. "Kyle, tell me what happened."

"The shelves fell on me," he said. "What the fuck do you think happened?"

"How did they fall?"

"I grabbed a box, and I think the bottom must have been busted. One of the flaps was under the shelves. When I picked it up, it must have caused the shelves to fall." He was trying to close his eyes, but she kept grabbing his arm and shaking him gently. She did not want him to fall asleep. His eyes popped open and he turned his head to look at her. "You have to call Erica. Oh, Jesus, she's going to be pissed."

"I'm sure she'll be worried, not pissed," Cass said. She heard sirens in the distance, and she closed her eyes in relief. They were getting closer. He was right though. She was going to have to get in touch with Erica. If they were going to have to do any kind of surgery on his leg, she'd have to sign the paperwork to grant consent.

She walked a few feet away and pressed the button on her phone to call Erica. After the fifth ring it transferred her straight to her voicemail system. For half a second, Cass considered hanging up, but what if Erica wasn't answering simply because it was her calling? If that were the case, then she could end up trying all day to reach her and never get an answer. The rational part of her brain knew Erica wouldn't ignore her call when Kyle was with her though. Besides, how would she feel if something had happened to Danny and the person trying to contact her didn't leave a message?

"Hey, Erica, this is Cass," she said with a quick glance toward Kyle, who was grimacing in pain. "There was an accident. I don't think it's anything serious, but some metal shelves fell on Kyle's leg. The ambulance is almost here, so I need to go. Call me when you get this, or I'll try you again later, when I have an update on his condition."

She disconnected and shoved the phone into her pocket before raking a hand through her hair. She would rather have actually spoken with Erica instead of leaving a rambling message including the words *ambulance* and *shelves fell on Kyle's leg*. Hearing it with no one to speak to, to ask questions of, was going to raise Erica's stress level through the roof. Especially with no explanation as to which hospital he was going to be taken to. Maybe she should have waited until they were at the hospital to call.

"Cass," Kyle said, his voice sounding weak. She hoped to God he hadn't hit his head when he fell. She crouched down next to him and put a hand gently on his shoulder. "When you talk to her, tell her I'm okay. She'll worry too much otherwise."

"You got it, buddy," she said. She didn't like the distant look in his eyes. The siren sounded like it was close, so she squeezed his shoulder before standing and walking toward the entrance to the unit. "You hang in there, Kyle. Help is almost here."

She saw the ambulance driving slowly through the facility so she ran out by the truck and began waving her arms in the air to gain the driver's attention. It seemed like mere seconds before they were inside the unit tending to Kyle. Cass watched as the two medics simultaneously hooked Kyle up to fluids, stabilized his leg so they could attempt to remove the metal protruding from his thigh, and were asking them both questions.

They both answered their queries as best they could, and it seemed as though a silent communication passed between the two medics. Apparently, they decided it would be safer for Kyle if they transported him the way he was and let the doctors worry about removing the metal. Cass couldn't say she was disappointed at the decision, because she was sure it would be painful. And messy. At least at the hospital they'd be able to knock him out before removing it. The kid was in enough pain as it was.

"Are you his mother?" one of the guys asked her when they had him on the gurney and started rolling it toward the ambulance.

"What?" she asked in surprise. She realized she *could* technically be his biological mother, but the thought struck her as funny and she forced herself not to laugh out loud at the question. "No, I'm—"

"Sister," Kyle said as he swiped at the guy's arm. When he looked down at Kyle, Kyle glanced over at Cass. "She's my sister. I want her to come with me."

Cass wanted to say no. She couldn't just leave the truck there. How the hell would she get home? She started to open her mouth but stopped when she really looked at Kyle. He was afraid. He was in pain. And he didn't want to be alone. How could she say no to him?

"Are you coming then?" the other guy asked her. "We need to get on the road."

"Yeah, just give me a few seconds." Cass ran out and made sure the truck was secured before doing the same with the unit. As she climbed into the back of the ambulance, the first guy motioned for her to have a seat near Kyle's head. She smiled at Kyle, hoping to allay his fear, and he grasped her hand with unexpected strength. She pulled out her phone with her free hand and willed Erica to call her back.

Chapter Twenty-six

Erica sat in her car staring up at the house she'd grown up in. She hadn't seen her parents since the day she came out to them, and the only time she'd spoken to either of them was when Kyle had shown up at her place out of the blue.

"Hey, you ready?" Lila asked from the passenger seat. They'd met at the mall a few minutes from there, and Erica hadn't said a word during the drive to the house in spite of Lila's attempts at small talk. "You can do this."

Erica wasn't so sure. The only thing she felt fairly certain about was that she was going to throw up. Hopefully not in the car, but maybe in her mother's flower bed. The thought caused her to let out a bark of laughter. When she looked at Lila, she laughed at the horrified expression on her face.

"I'm sorry," Erica said, but she wasn't. She felt better somehow, after imagining how her mother might react to finding the contents of her stomach in her flowers. It served as a good reminder that her parents were only human, after all. They were no better than she was, and she knew they couldn't hurt her unless she allowed them to. She took Lila's hand. "Are you ready? This can't be easy for you either, and I can't tell you how thankful I am you offered to come with me today."

"I'm here for you, Erica, and I need you to be here for me too," Lila answered. "If we present a united front, they won't have a choice but to listen to us. They can't hurt us."

They both nodded and got out of the car. They met in front of it and held hands on the way up the walk to the front door. When Lila reached out to ring the doorbell, Erica had the sudden urge to run away and never look back. She had a split second to realize her phone was vibrating in her pocket, but then the door flew open and she was standing face to face with her mother.

"What the fuck are you doing here?"

"Such nice language from someone who proclaims to be Christian, Tammy," Lila said with a quick squeeze of Erica's hand.

Erica took a deep breath in an attempt to center herself and then let it out slowly. Her mother looked like she was ready to grab a shotgun and run them off the property. It was a good thing she knew her parents were so against guns, otherwise she might think it was a real possibility.

"Hello, Mother. May we come in?" she asked, sounding more pleasant than she felt.

"No, you may not." She started to close the door, but Lila firmly placed a hand on it and held it open. "What do you think you're doing?"

"We're coming in whether you like it or not, Tammy," Lila told her in a tone Erica knew left no room for argument. "We don't want to be here anymore than you want us to be here, trust me. And the sooner you let us in, the sooner we can be done and on our way, surely never to darken your door again."

Erica's mother looked pissed. Erica didn't know where all this anger came from, because both of her parents had been rather laid-back and easygoing while she was growing up. She watched as her mother shook her head but motioned them inside.

"Where is my dear brother?" Lila asked.

Erica followed them into the kitchen where they all sat around the table. She could use some coffee, but she wasn't about to ask for any. Besides, she was certain her mother wouldn't make any for her anyway. Erica did her best to ignore the jab of pain in her heart at the depth of the hatred her mother apparently harbored for her.

"Ronnie isn't home from church yet. It was his turn to teach Sunday school, and it always runs a little longer than the regular service."

"Now there's a scary thought," Lila murmured under her breath so Tammy couldn't hear her. Erica did though, and she coughed into her hand to cover up the smirk on her face. "Will he be home soon?"

Tammy—because Erica had a hard time thinking of this woman as her mother any longer, so it was only fitting she thought of her by her given name—glanced behind her at the clock on the stove and shrugged before turning back to them.

"He should be here in a few minutes. He won't be happy to see either of you, you know."

"He couldn't be any less happy to see us than you were," Erica said.

"Why are you here?" Tammy asked. She had a look of disgust on her face as she spoke to Erica, and Erica tried not to flinch as she pinned her with her eyes. "I think we made it pretty clear to you we never wanted to see you again."

"You did," Erica said with a nod. She looked down at her hands folded in her lap and came to a decision. She was through allowing her mother to treat her this way. She raised her head and sat up straighter. "What did you tell the neighbors? Do they think I just left and never call you, or did you tell them I died?"

Tammy recoiled at that, though if it were the words themselves that caused the reaction, or the tone Erica used, she wasn't sure. Erica was pissed, and she was done trying to appease anyone. They'd turned their backs on her, and she'd accepted it. But now they were doing the same thing to her brother, and sitting here in the kitchen of the house she'd grown up in brought all of her anger to the forefront.

"We don't have children anymore," Tammy said. "You both strayed from God's path, and we cast you out. Have you changed your ways?"

Erica laughed at the hopeful look in Tammy's eyes. She thought it was ludicrous they were even having this conversation.

"It isn't something I can change about myself any more than you could change it about yourself." Erica noticed her leg was bouncing, and she stopped it. The nervous tic was something she thought she'd gotten rid of. "And even if I had, I still wouldn't want anything to do with either of you."

"Then why the hell are you here?" Tammy asked.

All three of them jumped when they heard the front door open. The kitchen wasn't visible from the door, so Erica knew he'd have no idea who was there. She smiled nervously at Lila, who took her hand once more and held it tightly. Neither one of them was looking forward to this.

"Tammy, hon, who's car is in the driveway?" he asked, sounding rather pleasant. "You didn't tell me we were having company this afternoon."

Erica braced herself when she heard his heavy footsteps coming toward the kitchen. When he rounded the archway and saw the three of them at the table, he almost stumbled over his own feet. He managed to keep his balance, but Erica noticed his face was turning a pretty shade of purple as he looked first at her and then at Lila, trying oh so hard to keep his anger under control.

"Get out of my house. You're not welcome here." He was shaking, and Erica found herself wondering if he might have a stroke.

"Sit down and shut the hell up, Ron," Lila said, sounding bored. "Listen to what we have to say, and then we'll be gone, and you'll never have to see either of us ever again."

"Did the neighbors see them?" Ronnie asked, taking a seat next to Tammy.

"So you did tell them I died," Erica said with a wry smile directed at Tammy. "How sweet. You know what? I hope they did see me. But just to make sure, I think I might go knock on a few doors before we leave and let your neighbors know how you treat your own children."

"If you so much as—"

"Calm down," Erica said, effectively shutting him up. "I wouldn't care so much if it was just me, but Kyle's still a kid. How could you treat him that way?"

"He shamed this family, Erica," Ronnie said, shaking his head the entire time he was speaking.

"How?" she asked. "By being honest with you about who he is?"

"You mean *what* he is," he said.

"No, I don't, but please, go on and show us the full force of your ignorance."

"You will not speak to me that way. I'm your father, damn it!"

"Not so much," Erica told him with a quick shake of her head. "You don't have any children anymore. Am I right, Tammy? You can't have it both ways, so I will talk to you any way I damn well please. Tell me how Kyle shamed you."

"He's slept with other boys. He's an abomination, just like you."

Erica leaned back in her chair, completely dumbfounded. She couldn't have formed words now even if she'd wanted to. She was afraid she'd string together enough profanities to make a sailor blush. Lila squeezed her arm, forcing Erica to look at her. Lila leaned close and spoke into her ear.

"Say what's on your mind, sweetie," she said. "You're never going to change the way they feel, but you might be able to give them a few things to think about."

Erica nodded as Lila relaxed back into her own space. Her heart was beating abnormally fast, and Erica took a few deep breaths to try to relax. She looked at her father who was sitting there with a self-righteous smirk on his face, his arms crossed defiantly over his chest.

"Kyle hasn't had sex," Erica said.

"Then how could he possibly know he's gay?" Tammy asked, her voice tight with what Erica thought was emotion, but more likely it was her way of controlling her own anger at what she saw as ignorance in Erica.

"Oh, my God," Lila muttered and shook her head.

"Did you have to have sex in order to know you were straight?" Erica asked, doing her best to keep her voice calm and not sounding like she was accusing them of something. When she looked at Ronnie she almost laughed. His mouth was moving, but there were no words coming out. He was turning purple again too.

"What a ridiculous question." Tammy slammed her hands down on the table and stood, apparently thinking her full height of five-foot-nothing was intimidating. "We're all straight until we choose not to be."

"So we're back to it being a choice," Erica said. "Because I would surely *choose* to be treated this way by my own parents. And it's pretty much a no-brainer that Kyle, knowing how you reacted when I came out, would *choose* to go through the same thing, right?"

"Maybe we're all gay until we choose not to be," Lila said. "Have you ever thought about that?"

Erica opened the file folder she carried in with her from the car and slapped the papers the lawyer had given her on the table, turning them so they were facing her parents. She shoved them at her father.

"I came here hoping to talk some sense into you, but I never dreamed how wrong I could be," she said. She was certain she could actually feel her blood pressure rising as she spoke. "But I realize now there are no circumstances in which I would ever want you involved in my, or Kyle's, life. So just fucking sign these papers and you'll truly be childless."

"What is this?" Ronnie asked, looking at her instead of the papers.

"It says you're waiving all parental rights where Kyle is concerned, therefore allowing me to become his legal guardian." Erica stood because she couldn't bear to sit still for another second. She began pacing while Ronnie glanced over the papers before signing. Once Tammy had done the same, he handed them back to her. After shoving them back into the folder, she motioned for Lila to follow her to the door, but she stopped before leaving the kitchen, causing Lila to almost run her over. "You know the saddest part in all of this? I grew up happy. I was under the assumption my parents loved me unconditionally. I wanted a family just like the one I grew up in. Now, I don't want to be anything like you. I feel sorry for you both because you stopped loving me the second you found out I loved another woman. You hate me because I love another human being. How pathetic is that?"

She left the house without another word, not comprehending exactly how much adrenaline was coursing through her until her knees almost gave out in front of the car. Lila was by her side instantly, an arm around her waist, holding her up.

"Come over here and sit in the passenger seat. I'll drive."

Erica was shaking so badly she didn't think she could drive at all. Once they were out of the neighborhood, she remembered her phone had been vibrating right before her mother opened the front door. She pulled it out of her pocket and was surprised to see she had four missed calls. All from Cass. And she'd left a message all four times.

"Fuck, what now?" she asked as she called her voicemail. Before it connected, the phone started vibrating in her hand. Cass was calling again. She answered, not at all sure she was prepared for what she was about to be told.

Chapter Twenty-seven

Cass was preparing herself to leave a voice message, *again*, as soon as she hit the call button on her phone. She gazed around the waiting room she was seated in and tried not to think about the people crying a few feet away from her who had just gotten news their loved one didn't make it through surgery. She turned her head and closed her eyes, and was shocked when Erica actually answered this call.

"Oh, thank God," Cass said with an audible sigh of relief. "Where are you?"

"I'm in Syracuse," Erica told her. "What's going on?"

"Didn't you listen to the messages I left?" Cass couldn't keep the exasperation out of her voice. What the hell was in Syracuse that could be more important than Kyle?

"I was just about to when you called, so just tell me what's going on." Erica sounded defeated. Cass chose not to ask what she was doing almost four hours away from Buffalo while her brother was in surgery.

"There was an accident," Cass told her.

"Oh, my God," Erica said, sounding appropriately worried now. "Is Kyle all right? Are you? What happened?"

"Some shelving fell on Kyle in the unit we were cleaning out. He has a broken leg, and he's in surgery right now." Cass winced at the sound of Erica's intake of breath. "They needed to get him in right away because a piece of metal went through his thigh. Apparently, it was really close to his femoral artery, and they needed to repair things before it got any worse."

"Is he going to be okay?"

"What's happening?" a voice asked. A woman's voice.

Of course Erica was spending the day with her new girlfriend. And why shouldn't she? Cass leaned forward in her chair and rested her head in her hand as she listened to Erica telling the other woman what Cass had already told her.

"Is he going to be all right, Cass?" Erica asked again after a few seconds of relaying information.

"The doctor says there's no real reason to think he won't be just fine." Cass wanted to ask about the woman she was with, but it wasn't any of her business.

"How is he in surgery without consent?"

"He told everyone from the medics on scene to the ER doctor to the surgeon who came to look at him that I was his sister. I didn't deny it, so they had no reason to think he was lying." Cass took a deep breath and braced for Erica's response. "I gave them consent to operate. It was a matter of life and death, according to the surgeon. I couldn't wait for you because I had no idea where you were, or how long it would be before I heard from you. I made an executive decision."

"Thank you," Erica said, and she started to cry. Cass wished she was there to comfort her. "Thank you for being there with him. I'll get there just as soon as I can."

Cass gave her the information concerning which hospital they were at, where it was, and where the waiting room she was in was located. She assured her she would call her back if he came out of surgery and was in a room before she got there. Cass was about to hang up when Erica spoke again.

"Are you all right, Cass?"

"Sure. I'm fine," Cass told her. She was, now that Erica finally knew what was happening. She'd been anything but fine before actually speaking with her. They hung up, and Cass experienced the strangest feeling of sadness. No one had ever been concerned about her like that before, but it didn't really matter, did it? Because being with Erica wasn't in the cards now that she had a girlfriend. She desperately wished she could go back in time and change how things between them transpired.

❖

"Lila, you missed the exit for the mall," Erica said as she watched it go by. Lila hadn't even slowed down.

"You really think I'd let you drive after getting such a phone call?" Lila asked, giving her a quick glance.

"But your car is there."

"I can get it later. There are more important things to worry about right now. I have friends who can get it for me so it won't get towed. We need to get you to Buffalo so you can be with Kyle." Lila changed lanes and sped past the line of slow moving vehicles. "Besides, I want to meet this Cassidy Holmes. She sounds like a real keeper."

"Yeah," Erica said quietly. She allowed herself a moment to think of the possibilities, but then came back to reality. "Too bad she doesn't think the same about me."

"Maybe you need to make her see it." Lila looked in the rearview mirror before moving back into the right-hand lane. "Have you told her how you feel?"

"I told her I'd be willing to take whatever she could give me."

"So you haven't told her you love her?"

"What?" Erica looked at Lila and was about to protest, but realized maybe she was right. Was it possible she loved Cass? Did it really make a difference in the grand scheme of things if Cass wasn't capable of returning her love? Or, more precisely, *willing* to? "No. I haven't."

"You should. The best things in life are worth fighting for, honey, and I'd say she qualifies for that statement."

Erica stared out the window as they talked for a few more minutes, trying not to think about what had transpired between her and her parents, while at the same time trying not to think the worst about what Kyle was going through. When her phone rang, it startled her.

"Cass?" she said into the phone after fumbling it and dropping it at her feet.

"He's out of surgery and doing fine. He's in recovery now, but should be transferred to a room in just a few minutes," Cass told her. "I'll call again when I know the room number. I just wanted to let you know he was okay."

"Thank you," she said. The nap had helped, but she still felt exhausted after the events of the day. "You'll still be with him when I get there, won't you?"

Cass hesitated, and Erica started to worry she didn't want to see her.

"Please?" Erica asked. Cass sighed into the phone before agreeing to wait for her. "Thank you again. I'll be there soon."

"Yep," Lila said with a nod as Erica disconnected the call. "She's definitely a keeper."

❖

"How are you feeling?" Cass asked when Kyle opened his eyes and turned his head to look at her.

"Like I was hit by a truck," he responded, his voice scratchy. "Where's Erica?"

"I just talked to her to let her know your room number, and she should be here in a few minutes." Cass stood and went to the side of his bed.

"What time is it? Why is it taking her so long to get here?"

"She was out of town," Cass told him. "But she's on her way."

"Syracuse?" he asked, surprising Cass.

"Yeah."

He closed his eyes again and turned away from her. She wanted to ask what was wrong, but when she saw his shoulders shake with an obvious sob, she decided maybe she shouldn't. She was relieved when she heard the door to the room open, and turned to see Erica walking in. The other woman was right behind her. Cass stepped away from the bed to give them better access.

"Oh, Kyle, are you all right?" Erica asked.

It was obvious to Cass that Erica had been crying. When the other woman turned her head to smile at Cass, Cass decided she had to leave. Without a word, she walked out of the room and down the hallway before ducking into the restroom to try to pull herself together.

CHAPTER TWENTY-EIGHT

Cass, I don't know how to thank you," Erica said as she turned. But Cass wasn't there. She looked at Lila who shrugged.

"She was here a minute ago."

"You should go find her," Kyle said, acting as if he didn't want to see her. Could he be this pissed because she didn't get there sooner?

"Kyle, are you mad at me?" Erica could tell he'd been crying, even if there weren't still tears on his cheeks. His eyes had the puffiness of a recent cry.

"Why were you in Syracuse?" he asked. "Were you trying to talk them into taking me back?"

"What? No, Kyle," she said, reaching out to brush the hair out of his eyes. "I had papers I needed them to sign in order to go forward with the guardianship. I'd hoped they wouldn't completely cut you out of their lives, but I wouldn't have let them force you home even if they'd wanted you back."

He nodded and seemed to be relieved at her words. She squeezed his shoulder and smiled at him. Lila took his hand and tilted her head toward the door, indicating Erica should go and find Cass. She shook her head. Even though she wanted to talk to her, she couldn't leave Kyle so soon after arriving.

"Go," Lila said. "I'll stay here with him."

"I promise I won't go anywhere while you're gone," Kyle added with a goofy smile.

Erica laughed at them both and turned to head toward the door. She didn't know how long Cass had been gone, or where she'd headed, but she had to find her. Lila was right. She needed to tell Cass how she felt. She looked both ways down the hall and saw the sign for the ladies' room. She was sure she looked a mess and decided washing her face might be a good thing before facing Cass. She stopped dead in her tracks when she saw Cass standing at the sink, staring at her own reflection. Her eyes moved to look at her, and she smiled sadly.

"Hi," Cass said before turning away from the mirror and facing her.

"Hi." Erica forced herself to walk toward the sink but stopped a few feet away from Cass. "I can't thank you enough for being with Kyle today."

"I thought you'd be mad." Cass looked relieved and Erica fought the urge to take her in her arms and kiss her.

"Why? It was an accident. You took care of him, and I appreciate it," Erica said. She wondered why Cass kept looking at the door. "Why did you leave the room?"

"I couldn't stay there," Cass said, folding her arms over her chest and looking down at the floor. "Not with her there."

"Who?" Erica asked, feeling a little surprised. "My aunt Lila?"

"She's your aunt?" Cass sounded dubious as her head snapped up, and Erica couldn't help but smile. Was it possible Cass was jealous? "I thought she was your girlfriend."

"I'm sure she'll be flattered to hear that, but she's my father's sister, and she's twenty years older than me, Cass."

"Then she's not your girlfriend?"

Erica shook her head and closed the distance between them. Cass's cheeks were flushed and she stood up straight as Erica cupped her cheek, rubbing her thumb slowly along her jaw. Erica felt the arousal start deep in her belly when Cass's pupils dilated.

"I don't have a girlfriend." Erica didn't resist when Cass placed her hands on her hips and pulled her close. Their kiss was slow, full of promise, and Erica let herself melt into it.

"Oops, sorry," came a voice from behind them.

Erica pulled away and saw a nurse standing in the doorway, a smile on her lips. Cass looked at them both before pushing her way past the nurse and disappearing down the hall. Erica sighed in frustration.

"I didn't mean to interrupt," the nurse said.

Erica waved off the woman's apology and went after Cass, who she saw walking into Kyle's room. At least she wasn't leaving. She took a moment to catch her breath before following her.

Cass hung around for a little while, but it was getting late and she said she had to go. Erica offered to give her a ride to her truck, but Cass declined, saying she should stay with Kyle.

"Are you sure?" Erica asked, disappointed she hadn't had more time alone with her. "It's no problem, really."

"I'll call you tomorrow," Cass promised before walking out the door.

"You didn't tell her, did you?" Lila asked after she was gone.

"Tell her what?" Kyle asked, causing Erica to jump. She'd thought he was asleep.

"She loves her," Lila answered.

"It's about time," he said. "All it took was me getting impaled by a piece of metal."

"I'm right here, guys," Erica told them, but they ignored her.

"I think Cass loves her too," Kyle said.

"That was pretty apparent by the way she was looking at her." Lila chuckled.

"I know, right?"

"Okay, enough," Erica said as she stood from her chair. She sighed, wondering if she could catch up to Cass if she left now, but decided against it. She just hoped Cass intended to keep her word and call her the next day.

❖

When Erica emerged from her bedroom the next morning, Lila was eating breakfast. She walked past the table and went right for the coffee pot.

"Good morning," Lila said, looking up from the newspaper she was reading. "How did you sleep?"

"Not particularly well," she answered, taking a seat across from her and eying the paper suspiciously. "You didn't steal the newspaper from the neighbor, did you?"

"They'll never know it was me," Lila said with a wink. "Did she call yet?"

"It's only eight o'clock in the morning," Erica said. "She probably isn't even up yet."

"Maybe you should call her."

"No. I'll wait. She said she'd call."

"I'm just saying. At least if you call her, you won't have to put up with your stomach being tied up in knots all day."

Erica sipped from her coffee and ignored Lila. It wasn't like the same thought hadn't crossed her mind when she'd woken up, but she was determined to wait it out. Cass said she'd call, and there was no reason not to believe her.

"I don't know how to thank you for yesterday, Lila."

"It was no problem," she answered. "Any of it. Once you told me you were going to Syracuse to face your parents, there was no way I was going to let you do it alone after the way they treated me. And you were in no shape to drive after hearing what happened to Kyle. I was just glad I was around to help. You know you can call me anytime you need me, right?"

"I do know, and I thank you," Erica said. It was strange how family dynamics could play out sometimes. After the previous day, she knew in her heart her father would never change his views, and even though they did what she wanted by signing off on their parental rights, it still cut deep. She was just happy to be done with them, and to know Lila always had her back. "How long are you going to stay?"

"I'm leaving today," Lila answered. "I'll hitch a ride with you to Buffalo when you go to see Kyle, and take the bus back to Syracuse to retrieve my car."

"You're more than welcome to stick around for a few days."

"I called out sick today, so I have to get back to work tomorrow, and you don't need an old woman cramping your style if things heat up between you and Cass."

"Please. Last night she thought you were my girlfriend. Maybe she's thought so since the night at Applebee's. I know she was there, and I'm pretty sure she saw us. That must be why she didn't come over to say hello." Erica thought for a moment before repeating herself. "She thought you were my girlfriend."

"Thank her for me, will you?" Lila laughed out loud and shook her head. "I was never quite sure how the plastic surgery came out, but if she thinks I look young enough to hold your attention, I'm convinced it worked like a charm."

"It did, trust me," Erica said. "And even if it didn't, you're barely over fifty, and I still don't think you needed any work done anyway."

"Thank you, but now that she knows who I am, she might just be ready to make her move."

Erica nodded as she considered the possibility. Even if Cass wasn't ready to make a move, Erica decided she might just make it instead.

CHAPTER TWENTY-NINE

He's going to be okay though, right?" Cass's mother asked as they were almost done eating breakfast.

Everyone had been asleep when Cass finally got home from the hospital the night before, so she'd gone right to her cabin. This morning over breakfast, she relayed the incidents of the previous day to all of them.

"That's what the doc said," Cass answered with a shrug. "I'm just glad Erica finally got there. I was so freaking strung out by the time he was done in surgery."

"And where was she all day?" Barb asked. She leaned over to wipe some baby food off Rance's face as she spoke.

"Syracuse."

"Why?" Danny asked.

"She's from there," Cass said. "I assume she went to see her parents for some reason."

"But I thought you said they didn't want anything to do with her or Kyle," her mother said. Cass could tell she was itching to give her own personal commentary on what exactly she thought of people who would turn their backs on their kids, no matter what their reasoning, but she opted to keep it to herself. Cass was thankful.

"That's what she told me, but I'm assuming it had something to do with her becoming Kyle's legal guardian. Forgive me, but

I didn't think it was the right time to ask her why she went to Syracuse." Cass sat back in her chair and pushed her plate away from her. Barb really did make the best pancakes in the world, but Cass had the tendency to gorge herself on them. "I told her I'd call her today, so maybe I'll ask her about it then."

"So, the woman there with her was her aunt?" Barb asked, barely managing to keep from laughing, which was obvious by the way she covered her mouth and refused to look at Cass.

"Maybe you would have known that if you'd bothered to talk to her at any point during the past three weeks or so," Danny added. Cass glared at him before slugging him in the shoulder. "Damn it!"

"Stop it, both of you," their mother said, raising her voice. "I raised you better."

Danny stuck his tongue out at Cass, and she responded by kicking his shin under the table. Rather than risk being yelled at again, he got up and refilled his coffee, rubbing his shin with a grimace as he did so.

"But he's right, dear," her mother said. "You should have just talked to her."

"Ha ha, told you so," Danny said in a singsong voice from across the room.

Cass started to get to her feet, but her mother put a firm hand on her forearm and shook her head. Frustrated, Cass folded her arms over her chest.

"Daniel," Barb said, and Cass barely stopped the snicker from erupting into a full-blown laugh. Cass only called him by his given name when she was pissed at him, but Barb only did it when she was ready to take his head off, and he knew it. His shoulders sagged as he went to stand next to Barb's chair. "Take Rance upstairs and change his diaper for me."

"Yes, dear," he muttered. They all watched while he unstrapped Rance from his highchair and picked him up, wrinkling his nose in disgust when he realized what was in the diaper. To his credit, he didn't complain, but simply walked out of the kitchen with Rance in his arms.

"When you call her are you going to tell her you love her?" Barb asked, looking rather smug.

Really? This was why she made Danny leave the room? So she and her mother could grill Cass about her feelings and intentions? She shook her head and opened her mouth to tell Barb she had it wrong, but she didn't. Cass felt like a freight train hit her at the realization. When exactly had love snuck up and bit her in the ass?

"No," she said firmly.

"But you do, don't you?" her mother said, more of a statement than a question. Cass looked at her for a moment before finally nodding. "Then you should tell her."

"I will, but it isn't really something you tell someone over the phone for the first time, is it?"

"Oh, you really are a romantic at heart, aren't you?" Barb asked, but her tone didn't indicate teasing, and it made Cass uncomfortable. "I think it's sweet."

Cass got up without another word and left through the sliding glass door so she could go back to her cabin. She didn't want to have this conversation with them. She wanted to talk to Erica, and she didn't want to wait until later, when Erica would probably be at the hospital visiting Kyle.

After letting Gordy out to do his business, she made herself a cup of coffee and sat on the couch, cell phone in hand, and realized her heart was beating rather fast. What if Erica didn't feel the same way about her? She remembered the kiss they started in the restroom at the hospital the night before and knew without a doubt that was one thing she didn't have to worry about. The kiss had been full of promises of things to come, a kind of kiss Cass never experienced before. She smiled as she scrolled through her contacts to find Erica's name.

"Hello?" Erica said.

Cass closed her eyes and let the sound of Erica's voice wash over her for a moment. Her lips tingled with the memory of their last kiss.

"Cass? Are you there?"

"I'm here, sorry," she answered, opening her eyes and resting a hand on Gordy's back as he lay curled up beside her. He lifted his head to look at her, but when she didn't acknowledge him, he rested his chin on his paws and went back to sleep.

"Are you okay?" Erica sounded worried.

"I'm fine." Cass could hear Lila in the background asking Erica something, but then she heard a door close. Apparently, she'd gone into her bedroom to have some privacy. "Are you okay?"

"Yes, thanks for asking."

This was awkward, and Cass hadn't expected it to be. Maybe things between them hadn't really changed, and she was surprised to feel disappointment at the thought.

"When will you be going to see Kyle today?" Cass asked.

"We were getting ready to leave in just a few minutes."

"Oh. I don't want to keep you."

"No, you aren't," she said quickly. She sounded like she was smiling, if that was even possible. It made Cass's heart swell. "I was hoping you'd call."

"I said I would," Cass answered. Lame. Now she'd think it was the only reason she was calling. "I was wondering if you might want to have dinner with me tonight. You can choose the restaurant."

"I would love to."

"Great. Can I pick you up around six?"

"Six sounds perfect. I'll spend the morning and early afternoon with Kyle, and I should be home in plenty of time."

"If you decide to spend more time with him, it's okay," Cass said. "We can do it another time."

"No, I doubt I'll want to spend even that much time in the hospital, but I know he'll be bored out of his mind. He'll understand."

"Well, just give me a call if you change your mind."

"I won't." Erica sounded sure, and Cass relaxed a little. "I hope you won't change your mind."

"Not a chance," Cass answered. "I've missed you, Erica."

"Me too," she replied. "Missed you, I mean."

"Okay, I guess I'll see you tonight. Tell Kyle I said hello."

They hung up, and Cass sat there motionless for a few minutes after ending the call. She was about to take a leap she thought she'd never take, and instead of scaring her, it actually felt liberating.

Chapter Thirty

"Why are you here?" Kyle asked, looking much better than he had the night before. Erica had just told him about her dinner plans for the evening. "You should be at home getting ready for your date."

"Kyle, it isn't even noon yet," Erica said with a grin. "I hope you don't think it would take me that long to get ready to go out."

"You never know. It always seemed like it took forever for Mom to get ready to leave the house."

"I'm not Mom," Erica said, and they both sobered at her words.

"Thank God," Kyle muttered. After a moment, he smiled again. "So they really signed the papers? You're going to be my legal guardian?"

"It looks that way," Erica said. "But it means they'll have nothing to do with you again."

"That's cool. I've kind of realized in the past few weeks I didn't really know them." Kyle looked sad, but only for a fraction of a second. "Maybe Cass will want to be my guardian too."

"Slow down, buddy. I don't even know where this might lead between us. I doubt she's changed her mind about wanting anything long-term, so don't get your hopes up." Erica had worried about this since she'd talked to Cass earlier. The fact was, Erica had given up hope of finding a relationship like her parents had, because like Kyle, she now felt as if she never really knew them. And Kyle was so obviously enamored with Cass, she knew he'd be the one making long-term plans.

"You guys will be married by the time I go off to college," he said, looking utterly sure of himself. Erica smiled and shook her head. "Trust me; I know these things."

"We'll see. I'm not making any promises about anything." Erica looked at her watch, wondering what time she would have to leave in order to get home and shower in time for Cass to pick her up at six. But then an idea struck, and she stood from the chair she'd been occupying and placed a hand on Kyle's shoulder. "Would you be terribly upset if I left? I think maybe I'll make dinner for her instead of letting her take me out to eat."

"Good thinking," Kyle said with a wink. "That way you never have to leave the house, and hopefully she'll be there in the morning too."

"You must be feeling a lot better today. You're back to being your usual pain in the ass." Erica kissed him on the cheek before ruffling his hair.

"I'm just saying, I won't be there, so that has to be something in your favor, right?"

"I'll see you tomorrow. Try not to give the nurses a hard time."

"You're no fun," she heard him say as she walked out the door.

She just hoped she had enough time to get to the store and have dinner ready by six.

❖

Cass was about to take Gordy up to Danny's for the evening when there was a knock at her door. She looked at her watch and cursed under her breath. She was running late and would have to speed in order to make it to Erica's by six. Gordy barked as she walked over and opened the door. It was her mother.

"I'm late, Mom. I don't have time for a pep talk," she said, clipping the leash on to Gordy's collar. Her mother took it from her and smiled.

"I came to get him because we knew you'd be running late," she said. She looked Cass up and down, and Cass fought not to squirm under the scrutiny. "None of us expect you home tonight, so don't worry about the dog. Just have fun."

"I intend to," she answered with a rakish grin. She dodged her mother's hand when she reached out to slap her on the arm. "But I'm sure I'll be home. We're only going out to dinner."

"Then why do you look so nervous?"

Cass was surprised her inner turmoil was obviously noticeable. She'd thought she was displaying the utmost confidence. If her mother could see it, then she was sure Erica would be able to as well.

"Come on," her mother said, walking into the cabin and shutting the door behind her. She unleashed Gordy and took Cass's hand, leading her to the couch. "Talk to me."

"What if I screw everything up?" There. She said it out loud. Well, it wasn't the first time she'd voiced the concern, but somehow she knew it wasn't the same when only Gordy was there to hear her.

"Trust me, Erica likes you. A lot." Her mother smiled and squeezed her hand briefly.

"How do you know?" Cass asked. "You've never even met her."

"True, but I've heard quite a bit about her from Barb, and you. From what I've heard, I have no doubt she likes you. Why do you have doubts?"

"I don't know," Cass said with a shake of her head. She did know, but she didn't want to tell her mother. Cass had never thought herself worthy of being loved. She'd convinced herself she was going to spend her life alone, and now that another path was becoming possible, she wasn't entirely sure how to deal with the onslaught of emotions.

"I think you do, but it's okay if you don't want to talk about it. Just be yourself. If I'm right, and she likes you, everything will work itself out, as long as you don't run away and hide from her again." Her mother cupped her cheek and smiled at her, and Cass felt the warmth of her mother's love she hadn't experienced in a long time. "You're happier now than I've seen you since I've been back, and if she can do that for you, then she must be a very special woman."

"She is," Cass said. "She really is."

They both stood and walked back to the door, and Cass clipped Gordy's leash back on to his collar. Before she left, her mother pulled her into an embrace.

"Let me tell you a secret," her mother said into her ear. "You know you're in love because you're nervous. If you weren't in love, then there'd be no reason to worry. Just promise me you'll tell her how you feel. And bring her home with you in the morning. I want to meet her."

"Mom, we're only having dinner," Cass said, feeling her cheeks flush. "I'll be home tonight. Alone."

"Sure you will." Her mother smiled and turned to walk away, Gordy followed her happily, his tail dancing back and forth as they went.

When Cass asked Erica to have dinner with her tonight, she'd intended it to be a date, but she knew she hadn't made her meaning clear over the phone. Because of that, Cass had tried her best to not think of tonight as a date, but she was having a hard time with it. The bottom line though, was whether Erica was going to consider it a date. If she didn't, there was no sense in hoping for more than dinner with a beautiful woman. But if she did…

"You're going to drive yourself nuts, Holmes," she said as she pulled her coat on and headed out the door. "Just show up and see where it goes."

Chapter Thirty-one

Erica checked the steaks one more time before looking at the clock and wondering why Cass wasn't there yet. It was almost ten after six. She tried not to let herself worry, but what if Cass changed her mind and simply decided not to show up? Somehow, she didn't think Cass would do something so callous. She'd call if she wasn't going to make it.

At a quarter past, her stomach was so tied up in knots she thought she might throw up, but then she thought she heard a car in the driveway, so she pulled the curtains back slightly. It was her. The dread she'd felt when Cass wasn't there right at six turned quickly into nervous energy. She removed the apron she'd donned to prevent any food splatter on her clothes and tossed it into the laundry room. After running a hand over her blouse and her slacks, she made her way to the door.

Even though she'd been expecting it, the knock caused her to jump, and she laughed at herself for feeling so anxious. It was just a date, right? Well, maybe it had been when she was supposed to pick a restaurant, but by opting to cook dinner at home, she took the guesswork out of whether or not she'd invite Cass in when she brought her home. She closed her eyes and took a deep breath before grasping the doorknob and twisting it.

"I'm so sorry I'm late," Cass said, and it was obvious to Erica how tense she was as well. "I got stuck behind a tractor on ninety-eight."

"They call that rush hour around here, don't they?" Erica asked, trying to sound calmer than she felt. Cass's grin told her she succeeded. Erica pushed open the screen door and motioned her inside. Cass stopped when the aroma of dinner reached her, and Erica found herself only a few inches from her.

"I thought we were going out?"

"Yeah, about that," Erica said, unable to move even if she'd wanted to. All she needed to do was lean forward and their lips would meet. She was about to do it when Cass took another step into the house and away from her, effectively breaking the spell. "I couldn't make up my mind about where I wanted to eat, so I stopped at the store on my way home from the hospital and picked up a few things. I hope that's okay with you."

"It's more than okay," Cass said. She pulled a hand from behind her back and held out a single red rose. "I hope this is okay."

"I can't think of any reason why it wouldn't be." Erica took it from her and held it to her nose, closing her eyes as she inhaled the wonderful scent. "It's beautiful."

"Just like you," Cass said.

Erica felt a slight flutter in her chest at the words. She didn't trust herself to speak around the lump in her throat, so she motioned for Cass to have a seat in the living room before she turned and headed for the kitchen.

"Just so we both know what tonight is about," Erica said as she put water in a vase. She was about to place the rose in the vase when she felt firm hands on her hips. She turned and found herself gazing into Cass's eyes and being held in her arms. She'd intended to ask if this was a date, but there was no way she could speak when Cass was looking at her this way.

"Did I fail to make it clear I was asking you on a date?" Cass asked.

Erica felt her knees go weak when Cass's mouth met hers in a kiss filled with so much meaning. Erica slid her arms around her neck and held her body against Cass, their tongues dueling for dominance. Erica finally gave in and allowed Cass to take control.

She sighed into her mouth when Cass ran a hand up her side and cupped her breast. She whimpered when Cass pinched her nipple, and she moaned when Cass slid a thigh between her legs. Erica pressed herself against the firmness of her leg and forced her mouth away from Cass's lips. Not because she wanted the kiss to end, but simply because she needed to catch her breath.

"Hopefully, that will answer any questions about where I stand on what this evening is about," Cass said.

"Oh, it does," Erica said, pressing a hand to her own chest in a feeble attempt to slow her racing heart. "Good to know we're on the same page."

"The food smells wonderful," Cass said, almost as if the kiss hadn't carried the same effect for her as it had Erica, but Erica knew better. There was a slight tremor in Cass's hands, which was a dead giveaway. "What are we having?"

"Well, I couldn't decide between steak and seafood," Erica said as she forced herself to turn away from Cass to tend to the food. "So I picked up a couple of sirloins and lobster tails. I also have mashed potatoes and asparagus. Any objections?"

"It sounds amazing. And if it's half as good as it smells, I may just want you to cook for me every night."

"Go take a seat," Erica said, trying her best to not read anything into the words she'd just heard. "It's ready, so I hope you're hungry."

"I'm starving."

Erica wondered if it would be inappropriate to suggest retiring to the bedroom as soon as they were done eating.

❖

Cass placed her napkin on the empty plate in front of her and leaned back in her chair with a satisfied sigh. They hadn't really talked much throughout dinner, but that was okay. They'd each caught the other one staring more than once, and each time it happened, the heat seemed to rise substantially in the room.

"So much better than any meal we could have gotten at a restaurant," she said. Her words caused Erica's cheeks to flush, and Cass felt inordinately pleased with herself for having caused the reaction.

"Thank you."

Cass stood when Erica did and helped her carry the dirty dishes into the kitchen. She rolled her sleeves up and turned on the water before Erica said something.

"What are you doing?"

"Dishes?" Cass said in the form a question, because she thought it was fairly obvious.

"You don't have to do that," Erica said.

Cass shut the water off and turned to face her, her butt resting against the edge of the counter. She took both of Erica's hands in hers and smiled at her.

"You made dinner for me, which I should point out you didn't have to do either. Cleaning up is the least I can do to contribute to what was by far the best meal I've had in ages." Cass brought one of Erica's hands to her lips and held it there as they looked into each other's eyes. "Unless you have dessert too? Because it would be silly to clean up twice."

"Dessert?" Erica looked around the kitchen, probably trying to figure out what she could make on the spur of the moment. "I bought popcorn. I thought maybe you'd like to watch a movie."

"That sounds great."

"Good. You go find something to watch, and I'll straighten up a bit in here."

Cass thought about arguing the point, but decided against it. She went to the living room and began hunting for a DVD collection, but there weren't any to be found. She finally sat down on the couch and turned the television on, but the screen remained black and the words *no signal* appeared after a few moments.

"I think your cable is out," she said.

"I don't have cable."

"Your satellite is out then."

"No satellite either." Erica came and sat on the opposite end of the couch and grinned at what Cass figured was her obvious confusion. "I'm a cord cutter. I refuse to pay the outrageous prices those companies charge for their services."

"Then how do you watch television?" Cass was confused; she could admit it. Who didn't have cable these days?

They spent the next half hour talking about the advantages of streaming over the Internet as opposed to paying for cable. Apparently, she could buy a device to connect her TV to her Wi-Fi. And for a nominal fee, she could subscribe to a service that would allow her to watch most shows the day after they aired. On her television. Cass was amazed, and this was something she was going to have to look into. But tonight was about other things. More intimate things, if she was interpreting the kiss before dinner correctly.

Cass looked through the movies available digitally while Erica returned to the kitchen to microwave some popcorn. Cass sat up straight in the hope Erica would sit next to her when she returned, but she was disappointed when Erica made herself comfortable at the other end of the couch once again. And they had separate bowls for their popcorn.

"Why are you so far away?" She placed her bowl on the coffee table. "And I don't mind sharing. Popcorn, that is."

"I didn't want to be too pushy," Erica answered with a shrug.

"I thought the kiss before dinner served to negate any feelings of nervousness or indecision," Cass said. She pushed the button on the remote to start the movie she'd chosen. *Elena Undone.*

"I'm not sure I can do the friends with benefits thing," Erica said. She was looking everywhere but at Cass, and Cass decided to take pity on her.

"I'm not sure I can either. Not with you." She paused the movie during the opening credits and smiled when Erica looked at her, eyes questioning. "I've done a lot of thinking over the past few weeks, and I've managed to come to the conclusion that you make me happy."

"What are you saying?" Erica's voice shook, and Cass had the feeling she wasn't even aware she got up and came to sit next to her, their thighs pressed together.

"I'm saying you make me feel things I never thought I could feel. If you'd asked me a month ago if I was happy, I'd have said yes without even thinking about it." Cass took her hand and laced their fingers together. She'd expected to be nervous while making this declaration, but she wasn't. And it surprised her. She knew without a doubt this was where she belonged. "But these past three weeks, not talking to you, not knowing where we stood, I knew I hadn't really been happy until you came into my life."

"What are you saying?" Erica asked again, and Cass couldn't help but grin. Flustered Erica was cuter than hell.

"I'm saying, if you're interested, I'd like to give this a try and see where it takes us."

"You want a relationship? With me?"

"I do. Very much. Unless it isn't what you want." She pulled her hand away, not wanting to push Erica into something she wasn't ready for. Her pulse was pounding in her ears while she waited to hear her response. Luckily, Erica didn't make her wait long.

"It is what I want," she said, settling in next to Cass. She placed her head on Cass's chest, but then looked up at her before truly relaxing into Cass's body. "But we'll take it slow if that's all right with you. I wouldn't want to spook you."

Cass nodded her response but had to wonder—weren't they already taking it slow? If the way her body was reacting to Erica now was any indication at all, she was definitely ready to speed things up a bit.

Chapter Thirty-two

Erica had to wonder at Cass's choice in what movie to watch. The chemistry between the two women in the film was almost palpable, and she couldn't deny she was getting turned on sitting there in Cass's arms, her head resting on Cass's shoulder. Cass's breathing was quick and labored, and every once in a while she'd shift her hips, almost as if she were uncomfortable. Erica had enough. She sat up, grabbed the remote, and stopped the movie. She stood and held her hand out to Cass, who looked surprised.

"What's wrong?" she asked, but took her hand and allowed Erica to help her to her feet.

"I think I might implode if I don't get to touch you soon." Erica had never been so bold before with anyone, but with Cass it felt right. If she didn't take what she wanted, when she wanted it, Cass might very well drive her insane.

"Then what are we waiting for?" Cass put an arm around her waist and pulled her close before kissing her hungrily.

Erica allowed her body to mold itself to Cass, and she had the fleeting thought she could stay like this forever in Cass's arms and never want for anything again. Except for the fact she felt her knees going weak the more Cass's tongue slid along hers and her hands moved slowly up Erica's sides. When Erica had to come up for air, she placed her hands on Cass's shoulders and took a step back, needing the distance between them for her own sanity.

Without a word, Erica walked through the house, turning the lights off as they went, holding onto Cass's hand as though she might disappear if they weren't tethered together. She almost tripped over Willie in the doorway to the bedroom, but she pushed him aside gently with her foot and flipped the light switch on. Once Willie left the room, she shut the door and faced Cass.

"What happened to taking it slow?" Cass asked, looking at her with unmasked desire.

"Are you spooked?"

"Not in the least."

"Then I'd say we're moving at exactly the right pace." Erica reached for the switch again, but Cass grabbed her wrist and shook her head.

"I want to see you while I make love to you, Erica."

Erica preferred the lights off, but she realized she'd do anything to make Cass happy. She closed her eyes and enjoyed the feel of Cass's hands moving slowly up her sides, then across her chest before Cass began to unbutton her blouse. When Erica tried to pull Cass's sweater up, Cass stopped her.

"No, let me undress you," Cass said. Erica thought she might melt from the intensity of her gaze. "You've seen me naked. I want to see you."

Erica fought to hold still while Cass finished removing her blouse. Her skin felt the chill in the air when her upper body was exposed. Cass reached behind Erica and unclasped her bra. She heard Cass's breathing quicken when she eased the straps down Erica's arms, and her eyes slid down to take in the sight of her bare breasts. Her nipples tightened at the same moment Cass's eyes darkened with arousal.

Cass leaned down and took a nipple between her lips. Erica arched her back and held Cass to her breast with both hands.

"Oh, Cass," she murmured. The intensity of her own arousal was almost too much to bear. She let out a moan as Cass's teeth raked across her nipple. "More. Please."

Cass pulled away and reached between them to undo Erica's pants. She let them fall to the floor before shoving her fingers inside the waistband of Erica's panties and pushing them down as well, stopping when her face was even with the apex of Erica's thighs. Erica stepped out of her clothes and put her hands on Cass's shoulders.

"You are so beautiful," Cass said, looking up at her.

"I need to lie down," Erica said, feeling as though her legs would give out at any moment.

Cass stood again and, with her hands on Erica's ass, she lifted her off the floor. Erica's legs went around her waist, and Cass walked them both to the edge of the bed before setting her down. Erica watched as Cass removed her own clothing and then settled on top of her, one firm thigh pressing against her center.

"You feel so good," Cass said, her lips less than an inch away from Erica's. She pressed her thigh harder into her, and Erica couldn't help but slide against it. It felt so wonderful.

Erica felt the first sensations of her orgasm building, deep inside. It felt like a fire spreading from her core, and she made herself stop grinding against Cass's thigh. She desperately needed release, but she didn't want it to come so fast. She wanted to savor every second of their time together.

"Is something wrong?" Cass asked.

"No." Erica closed her eyes and shook her head. "I'm going to come if you keep doing that with your leg."

"You don't want to come?"

"I do, more than you know." Erica looked at her and felt her heart speed up. The look of desire in Cass's eyes was almost too much to handle. "I want you inside."

Cass eased her leg away from Erica's center and put a hand between them, gently parting her folds and easing her fingers inside of her. Erica gasped and pushed against her hand, causing Cass's palm to press against her clit. There was no slowing this down now. She held onto Cass tightly as the tendrils of fire exploded through her, starting deep in her belly and moving quickly down her legs. She cried out Cass's name as she ground herself against her hand.

When she couldn't stand it any longer, she grabbed Cass's wrist to still her movements, her eyes locking with hers. She gently pulled Cass's hand away from her, another orgasm ripping through her at the movement.

"Are you all right?" Cass asked as she settled in next to her and held Erica against her body. She placed a gentle kiss on her cheek, and Erica realized she was crying. "Did I hurt you?"

"No," Erica answered, her throat tight with emotion. This was so not like her, but maybe she needed this more than she'd known. She wiped the tears from her eyes. "You're amazing. I don't know why I'm crying."

"As long as you're okay," Cass said, the concern evident in her voice.

"I am." She turned her head and smiled at her. "I'm more than okay."

Erica pushed her onto her back before kissing Cass. Cass shivered when Erica put a palm on her chest and moved it slowly down her front, across her belly and stopping only when she reached the hair between her legs. Cass's legs fell open as Erica pushed two fingers inside of her, and their kiss deepened.

Cass moaned into her mouth, the feel of Erica's fingers inside of her more incredible than she'd anticipated. She moved her hips slowly in time with Erica's gentle thrusts. Erica broke their kiss and moved lower, her lips skimming across Cass's jawline and her throat, before finally settling in with a nipple between her lips. Cass arched into her and turned her head to the side, enjoying all Erica wanted to give her.

It only took a few moments, and some well-placed pressure on her nipple, for her climax to crash through her. Erica held tightly to her as she convulsed with pleasure.

"Think we should go back to the living room and finish the movie?" Erica asked with a hint of humor to her tone.

Cass laughed. Erica did too as she snuggled into Cass's side, Cass's arm around her shoulders. She placed a kiss on the top of Erica's head and sighed.

"If I thought you were serious, I'd say yes."

"You don't think I'm serious?"

Erica's chuckle indicated she wasn't, but Cass decided to play along.

"I don't want to be anywhere but right where I am," she said, then paused. She pulled her arm away and started to sit up. "But if you'd rather watch the movie, let's do it."

Erica held tight to her with a hand around her waist, pulling her back into a prone position. Cass didn't object when she straddled her waist and left a swath of wetness across her lower abdomen. In fact, Cass felt herself becoming aroused all over again.

"You aren't going anywhere, Cassidy Holmes," Erica said with conviction, which turned her on even more. "I'm not even close to being done with you."

CHAPTER THIRTY-THREE

Erica woke to the incredible sensation of Cass's warm body pressed tightly against her. She had an arm around Cass and tried to pull her even closer. Cass's deep even breaths was all Erica needed to hear to know she was still sound asleep. She raised her head up to look at the clock on the nightstand and groaned when she saw it was only three in the morning. They'd drifted off to sleep numerous times, only to awaken and reach for each other again. Erica smiled at the memories they'd created of their first night together.

Cass stirred against her, and Erica realized she'd been absently running her thumb across a nipple. She stopped, but Cass was obviously awake and pressing her ass against Erica's front, causing her arousal to spark again. Cass grabbed her wrist and brought it to her mouth where she kissed the palm of Erica's hand, moaning when Erica pushed back against her.

"God, I can't seem to get enough of you," Cass murmured, her voice husky. She held Erica's hand firmly against her chest, right between her breasts. "I want you again."

Erica felt like she couldn't breathe as emotion overtook her senses. She felt the overwhelming need to tell Cass what she was feeling. She was pressing her forehead against Cass's shoulder as she tried to stop the words she needed to say, at the same time knowing it was futile.

"I love you." There. It was out there. Cass didn't react at first, but then her movements stilled. Erica started to pull her hand away from Cass, but Cass gripped it tighter. "I'm sorry. I shouldn't have said that. You don't need to say it back."

She held her breath waiting for Cass's reaction, but she heard her start to laugh. It started as a deep rumble in her chest, and Erica tried to pull away again, only to have her hand brought back to Cass's mouth for another kiss.

"I don't know what reaction I was hoping to get, but I'm pretty sure you finding it funny wasn't it," Erica said, suddenly wanting to be anywhere but in bed with a woman who saw fit to laugh at her declaration of love. She should have known better than to hope Cass meant what she'd said the night before about wanting to try having a relationship.

"No, wait, I don't think it's funny," Cass said, scrambling to turn onto her back. Once she was, she gazed up at Erica with a look that stunned her.

"That's not how I'm seeing it."

"Listen," Cass said, caressing Erica's cheek with the backs of her fingers and never breaking eye contact. "I'm not laughing at what you said. Trust me."

"Then what?" Erica still wasn't sure she believed her, but Cass's next words took her breath away.

"I had to bite my tongue more than once last night because I wanted to say those words to you." Her smile caused a rush of warmth to infuse Erica's entire body. "I love you, too."

"Why didn't you say it?" Erica asked, her heart racing.

"I thought it might be too soon. Or that you wouldn't feel the same way." Cass looked so unsure of herself it made Erica want to cry. What had it cost Cass to keep her emotions so bottled up for so long? "I think it might have destroyed me if I said it and you didn't say it back."

Cass looked away from her, but Erica placed a hand on her cheek and forced her head back. Erica wanted to say so much, but she wasn't sure where to begin, and she wasn't going to say anything until Cass met her eyes. When she finally did, Erica pressed their lips together for a moment before taking a deep breath to try to calm her heart.

"You will never have to worry about me not saying it back." Erica caressed her cheek as she spoke, and she could sense Cass beginning to relax under her touch. "You are everything to me, and I didn't even realize it until I saw you that night in Applebee's and you completely ignored me."

"I didn't know you saw me," Cass said quietly. Erica watched as one corner of Cass's mouth curled up in an adorable half-smile. "I thought you were with a girlfriend."

"Aunt Lila thanks you for confirming her plastic surgery accomplished what she'd hoped for."

"I was jealous," Cass admitted. Erica didn't resist when she urged her onto her back and settled her body on top of her. "I'd never experienced that particular emotion before. I can't say I liked it very much."

"I promise you will never have a reason to be jealous, Cassidy Holmes," Erica said, her body responding when Cass pressed her thigh against her. "I can't imagine wanting anyone the way I want you."

"Good to know," Cass said before kissing her and then sliding a hand between her legs.

❖

When Cass woke again, the bedside clock brightly displayed the time as five thirty. She tried to go back to sleep because the feel of Erica spooning against her back was warm and inviting, but sleep wasn't going to come. She could feel Erica's breasts and the gentle puffs of air as she breathed, and she wanted nothing more than to wake her up. Again.

But Erica was up by this time most mornings, and the last time Cass had looked at the clock before they'd finally given in to exhaustion it was little more than an hour ago. No, the best thing to do was to just allow Erica to sleep. She carefully crawled out of the bed and picked up her clothes before heading to the bathroom to get dressed.

She was about to head out the front door when she decided to leave a note. It wasn't something she'd ever done in the past, but it didn't feel right to leave Erica's bed after they'd declared their love for each other. She also didn't want Erica to think she'd panicked and ran away. This was all so new for Cass, and she didn't want to screw it up. It all felt so right to her, like this was where she belonged.

She scribbled a quick note and left it on the bedside table so when Erica woke up and looked at the clock she couldn't miss it. Not able to resist, she leaned down and kissed her on the forehead before heading home.

She showered and changed her clothes before heading to the main house and decided she'd try her hand at making breakfast. It was almost seven, and she heard someone walking around upstairs, probably because the baby had been crying.

Danny and Barb usually made pancakes, especially on Sundays, but Cass decided to switch things up a bit since she knew any attempt she made would fall well short of Barb's pancake nirvana. She managed to find everything she thought she needed to make French toast and started in on the preparations. Before she could place the first slice of bread into the pan, Danny walked into the kitchen, rubbing his eyes and looking for all the world as if he had a killer hangover.

"What time did you get home?" he asked after a huge yawn. He scratched his head before pouring himself a big glass of orange juice. "Mom and I were up until almost three playing cards, and you weren't home yet."

At least that explained his sleepiness. She hadn't given much thought to what she'd say about getting home so early in the morning, and she certainly hadn't expected they would be up so late to know she hadn't made it back. No sense in lying though, right?

"I got home a little after six." She didn't turn from the stove, so she couldn't see his expression, but she heard him almost choke on his juice. She smiled to herself.

"You what?"

"I'm pretty sure you heard me, so I'm not going to repeat myself."

"You spent the night?"

"Technically, no, since I got home before any normal people would be out of bed on a Sunday morning." Cass flipped the bread over and finally turned around to face him.

"You never spend the night. Ever. I mean, seriously. *Never.*"

"You, Barb, and Mom finally got through to me. You should be happy."

Danny set his glass of juice on the table and seemed to notice for the first time what she was doing. He looked at the stove and then back at her, his confusion more than apparent. She laughed at him, mostly because she couldn't help herself.

"What the hell are you doing?"

"I'm making breakfast for everyone. Is that a problem?"

"It is if you don't know what you're doing, and trust me, I've known you long enough to know you don't cook. Again, *never.*" He sat at the table, shaking his head. "I won't protect you from Barb if you burn down the house. Or ruin her griddle."

"Really? Ruining the griddle is on the same level as setting fire to the house?"

"You don't know Barb and her griddle. She'll have a conniption fit if anything happens to it."

"I won't let anything happen to her precious griddle. Just because I don't cook doesn't mean I can't. I've watched Mom cook French toast enough. Seems fairly simple." She removed the bread from the griddle and put two pieces on a plate before setting it in front of him. "Taste it and tell me if it's okay to serve to everyone."

"What happens if I keel over?"

"Then I'll clean up all evidence I'd even tried to cook, and tell the cops I have no idea what happened to you."

"How in the world can you be in such a good mood so early in the freaking morning?" he asked, but he made no attempt to butter his French toast. Cass decided to do it herself. "You're acting really strange."

He reached out to try and place his hand on her forehead but she stopped him by threatening him with the butter knife.

"Keep your filthy paws to yourself."

"Did you bring Erica home with you?" he asked when he'd finally stopped laughing, no doubt it was humorous to him that he could ruin her good mood so easily.

Little did he know the high she was riding wasn't going to end anytime soon. At least it wouldn't if she had anything to say about it. But she was fine letting him think he got under her skin.

"I let her sleep." She finished pouring maple syrup on his plate and stood back to wait for him to taste it.

"She was still sleeping and you snuck out?"

"I didn't sneak out. I left a note."

"At the risk of hearing TMI, you two did…" He paused as he was obviously trying to come up with a word that wouldn't sound crude. He looked at her for help, but she just shrugged.

"You're on your own here, little brother." Cass heard more movement upstairs and went back to the stove to get more food ready for whoever would walk into the kitchen next.

"You had sex, right?" he finally managed to spit out.

"She's a big girl, sweetie," Barb said as she walked into the room. "She can do whatever she wants, though I'm sure she wouldn't want to talk to you about it."

Cass barely suppressed the laughter she felt building, because she knew before she even looked at him that his face would be a fairly deep shade of red. He'd always embarrassed easily, ever since he was a small child.

"If she were my brother she would without even thinking about it," Danny said.

Cass turned and placed a fist on her hip as she waited for Barb to defend her. Barb glanced at her and rolled her eyes before going over and slapping Danny on the back of his head. Without breaking stride, she continued on to the coffee pot.

"You're probably right, but you never seem to quite grasp the fact she's your sister, not your brother," Barb said, her back to him as she refilled Cass's cup before tending to her own. "This is something she would talk to her sister about, am I right?"

Cass did a double take and she heard Danny laughing as he stood to leave. Cass realized where this was going when she ran the words through her head, trying to process them. She had no sister, but Barb considered herself to be just that. Cass didn't want to kiss and tell, but she also knew Barb wouldn't give up until she knew everything. She found herself wishing she'd just answered Danny's question.

"Sit, and I'll finish breakfast after we talk." Barb pulled a chair out for her then occupied the seat Danny had vacated.

Cass weighed her options. She could bolt out the back door, but she wouldn't put it past Barb to run her down. Yes, she'd given birth not too long ago, but the woman could flat out run. Cass wouldn't stand a chance. After a second, she walked toward the living room and looked at the stairs to make sure her mother wouldn't be walking in on them, like Barb had done to her and Danny.

"Tell me the truth," Barb said when Cass settled in with her coffee mug between her hands. "It sucked, right?"

"What? No!" Cass couldn't hide the incredulity in her voice. Apparently, it was the response Barb was looking for, because the smirk on her face caused Cass to slam her mug down on the table. There was no way she could plausibly deny it now. Might as well own up to it. She leaned forward and lowered her voice in case Danny was lurking about. Or her mother. Wouldn't that just make the morning complete? "It definitely did not suck."

"Was it the best you've ever had?"

"Barb, come on." Cass felt her own cheeks burning now. "It was good, and that's all you're getting out of me."

"Want to bet?"

"I'm not doing this." Cass folded her arms over her chest and shook her head.

"Are you going to see her again?"

"Maybe."

"You're almost as infuriating as my husband."

Cass was surprised when Barb got up and went to finish making breakfast. Something was off. It wasn't like Barb to give up so easily. It made Cass worry for what would no doubt come later. She just prayed Barb wouldn't embarrass her in front of Erica.

A shudder ran through her body at the thought of it.

Chapter Thirty-four

Erica finished the dishes from the night before and looked at the clock. Eight o'clock. She was tired from being up most of the night, but it was a good tired, and she in no way regretted the reasons for her fatigue. Or her sore muscles. She reached into her pocket and smiled when her fingers brushed over the piece of paper she'd folded and put there when she'd gotten dressed. She pulled it out and read it again.

Erica,

To say I had a wonderful time last night would not only be a cliché, but it couldn't come anywhere near what I'm really feeling. I wanted to wake you up and bring you home with me, but you looked so peaceful as you slept. Also, I knew I'd never make it out of the bed if you were awake, and I'm sure you know why.

Call me when you're up and about. I have someone I want you to meet.

I love you. God, I hope I didn't dream the conversation we had in the middle of the night.

Cass

Her belly made a strange fluttering sensation as she reached for the phone to call Cass. She'd been dismayed when she found nothing but the note when she'd awakened, but the words Cass had written made her smile. And they still made her smile after reading it now, for about the tenth time.

"Good morning," Cass said when she answered the phone, her voice low.

There was the strange fluttering again. Erica put a hand on her belly and pressed on her abdomen as her eyes slid closed. She thought she could listen to Cass's voice forever.

"Good morning," she answered.

"I'm sorry I left you alone earlier, but I figured you needed the rest."

"And you didn't?"

"No, I did, but going back to sleep wasn't really an option after waking up with your naked body pressed against my back."

"Next time you aren't leaving the bed until we're both awake."

"If we're in bed together, and we're both awake, I think it's safe to say getting out of bed would be the last thing on our minds." Cass's words caused a rush of heat between her legs, and Erica whimpered as she crossed her legs in a pointless attempt to stop the arousal.

"Jesus," she murmured, and she heard Cass chuckle on the other end of the line. "You should be here. With me. Right now. In bed."

"Hold that thought for now, even though I'd like nothing more," Cass told her. "You've missed breakfast, but my mother wants to meet you. Can I pick you up in a few minutes?"

"I need to go see Kyle," Erica said, feeling a bit of panic set in. Her *mother?* She wasn't sure she was ready to meet her quite yet.

"You don't have to stay long. She's been bugging me about you for weeks. And she's only going to be here for a few more days before she heads back to Japan."

Erica groaned inwardly. No matter how much she wanted to, there was obviously no way in hell she could say no to Cass.

"All right, but I'll drive myself. Then I can just go to the hospital from there."

"Let me pick you up," Cass said. "I'll go with you to see him. Unless you don't want him to know about us just yet."

"I'm pretty sure he knew about us before we did." Erica couldn't help but laugh, and it made her inexplicably happy to hear Cass joining her.

"I think you're probably right," Cass replied.

"You're more than welcome to go with me, but it's pointless for you to drive here and pick me up," Erica said, knowing Cass's house was a little closer to Buffalo than hers. "I'll be there in twenty minutes."

After they hung up, Erica filled Willie's food bowl, cleaned out the litter box, and grabbed her keys before heading out the door. She was nervous to be meeting Cass's mother, but she realized it was only because she didn't have a mother of her own for Cass to meet.

❖

"Swear to me you won't do or say anything to embarrass me in front of Erica," Cass said to her mother after looking at the clock on the stove for what seemed like the tenth time since getting off the phone. Erica should be arriving any moment.

"If I had any naked baby pictures of you, they'd be spread out on the table here just waiting for her."

Danny laughed and Cass kicked him under the table without looking at him. He let out a yelp and grabbed his shin.

"Serves you right," Barb told him.

"Mom," Cass said, dreading how this meeting was going to go. Maybe if she'd ever brought someone home to meet her before she wouldn't be so anxious about it now.

"Don't worry, dear. I won't embarrass you."

Cass let out a sigh of relief and glanced at the clock again.

"When are you going to move in together?" her mother asked, sounding as though she were asking nothing more important than what they wanted for lunch.

Cass felt her heart leap into her throat and she knew her expression gave away her dismay by the way Danny was laughing again.

"Come on, husband," Barb said. She got to her feet and pulled him up too. "They don't need you here for this."

"But—"

"Thank you, Barb," Cass said. When they were gone, she looked at her mother again. "See, you can't say things like that around Erica."

"Why not?" her mother asked, looking surprised. "It's a valid question, isn't it?"

"No, it's not!"

"Did you tell her you love her?"

"Yes."

"Did she say it back?"

"She said it first."

"Well then, it's an extremely valid question," her mother said with a grin.

Cass rolled her eyes when she heard the doorbell ring. She stayed put, knowing Barb would answer it, and hoping to dissuade her mother from speaking to Erica at all.

"Please, Mom," she said. "Maybe it would be best if you didn't say anything."

"Like that's going to happen," her mother said with a smile as she patted Cass's hand.

Cass put her head down, resting her forehead on the arm she had on the table. This was not at all the way she wanted Erica to meet her mother. Ever since she'd woken up that morning, she'd been thinking about asking Erica to move into the cabin with her, but now it wouldn't seem like it'd been her idea at all.

"You seem far too awake for someone who was up all night having sex," her mother said quietly.

Cass whipped her head up to respond just as Erica walked into the kitchen. She was mortified, and she could feel her cheeks on fire. Her mother just laughed as she stood and went to introduce herself.

❖

"Your mother seems like a wonderful woman," Erica said when they were finally on their way to Buffalo.

"That's only because you don't really know her," Cass answered, wondering if Erica could tell she said it with affection. Her mother hadn't said anything at all to embarrass her, and she was forever grateful. And they both seemed to genuinely like each other, which had been a welcome outcome.

"It's obvious she loves you," Erica said. "So at least I have something in common with her."

Cass smiled. She looked out the passenger window at the fields where crops were just starting to grow. It was a long-awaited sign indicating winter was finally over.

"Are you going to tell Kyle about us?" she asked.

"Not if you don't want me to, but I think he'll know if we show up there together." Erica placed a hand on her thigh, and Cass covered it with her own.

"I think we should tell him," Cass said. "Unless you think we shouldn't. Maybe he won't be happy about it."

"When I told him we were having dinner together yesterday, he asked me if I thought you'd want to be his legal guardian too," Erica said.

Cass waited for the panic to set in, but it didn't. When she started to pull her hand away, Erica turned hers over and laced their fingers together.

"I'm not asking you to do that, all right? I'm just trying to tell you he definitely wouldn't have a problem with us being together."

Cass smiled and nodded as she gave Erica's hand a quick squeeze. It worried her to realize this all felt so natural. If she asked

Erica to move in, it really would be a ready-made family situation. And much to her surprise, the thought actually made her happy.

❖

"I'm glad you two finally came to your senses," Kyle said after they told him they were giving the relationship thing a go. He looked genuinely pleased, and it made Erica's heart swell in her chest. "It was getting exhausting constantly being in the middle of it all."

"Whatever," Cass said with a laugh.

"So, who's moving where?" he asked.

"Excuse me?" Erica asked, genuinely confused.

"Is she moving in with us, or are we moving in with her?"

Erica didn't know what to say. She looked at Cass, but Cass was staring at her shoes and was of no help at all. She looked back at Kyle, but he was just waiting expectantly for someone to answer his question.

"I think it's a little too soon for that, don't you?" Erica asked. She was surprised when Cass raised her head and looked at her. Had she and Kyle actually talked about this? Because Cass looked as though she was hurt by Erica's words. Erica turned her attention back to Kyle. "We just decided last night to see where this might go. It isn't something we've even talked about."

"Fine, but it isn't something you should wait too long for. Life is short."

"And this is something you've realized because of your near-death experience the other day?" Erica asked, her tone teasing.

"Exactly." Kyle nodded once to emphasize his point. He looked at Cass. "Don't you have anything to say about this?"

"I'd be lying if I said it hasn't crossed my mind," Cass said.

Erica stared at her. Was this really happening? Two days ago, she'd resigned herself to the fact they would never be on the same page as far as relationships went, and now this? Not that she would be opposed to moving in together, but she wondered if this was really what Cass wanted, or if she was only saying it to make Kyle feel better.

"But I don't think it's something anyone should rush into," Cass said as she took Erica's hand. "We'd need to talk about it and decide if it was right for all of us."

Kyle's smile lit up his whole face. Erica thought maybe it lit up the entire room. They stayed for another forty-five minutes and never once hit on the subject again. In fact neither of them brought the subject up on the drive back to Cass's either. They didn't talk about anything more exciting than the weather and how Kyle was due to be released from the hospital in two days, barring any complications. Erica agreed to come inside the cabin with Cass and promised herself she'd put the topic on the table. Somebody had to, right?

CHAPTER THIRTY-FIVE

Cass woke up at three thirty that afternoon, her arm around Erica, who had her head resting on Cass's chest. Her breathing was deep and even, indicating she was still asleep. Cass debated whether or not to wake her, because they needed to talk about what Kyle had brought up earlier. Erica tried when they'd gotten inside the cabin, but Cass had more pressing things on her mind. The fact they'd both fallen asleep shortly after spoke to how exhausted they both were.

Cass figured she'd appeal to Erica's practical side. Did it make sense not to live together? Cass didn't think so. She could see how this would end up. Because she couldn't seem to get enough of Erica, she knew she'd end up spending most nights at the trailer. She certainly didn't have anything against the trailer, but she loved this cabin with its vaulted ceilings and the loft for a master bedroom. She was pretty sure she wasn't going to give it up without a fight.

"Tell me what you're thinking so hard about," Erica said before placing a soft kiss on Cass's chest and pulling away to prop herself up on an elbow.

"Nothing," she answered.

"Right. You were so far away you didn't even know I'd woken up." The look of worry on her face alarmed Cass. "You aren't having second thoughts, are you? About us?"

"What? No, no." Cass sat up so her back was against the wall and took hold of Erica's hand. "I've never been more sure of anything in my life. I'm not going to lie, I thought I'd be scared to death about being in a relationship, but you really do make me happy. I feel complete when you're around. From the night I met you, I think I knew on some level that this was where we were headed."

"Even though you fought it every step of the way?" Erica reached out and brushed the hair from Cass's eyes.

"I think that's exactly why I fought it," Cass said. Speaking from the heart wasn't something she'd ever done before, but this was surprisingly easy. And she knew it to be true only because it was Erica she was talking to. "Once I finally let go, I realized this was exactly where I wanted to be. Where I *needed* to be."

Erica looked as though she was going to start crying, but she was obviously not going to let it come easily. She roughly swiped at the tears welling up in her eyes and leaned in to kiss her. When she moved away again, she was smiling.

"What are you trying to say?"

"I love you," Cass said with absolutely no hesitation. "And I don't want to waste another second of my time away from you. How would you feel about moving in with me here?"

Erica didn't say anything at first, and Cass began to panic. It was too soon to talk about living together. She should have just kept her mouth shut about it.

"What about Kyle?"

"What about him?"

"We're pretty much a package deal, you know."

"I do know," Cass said with a slight grin.

"This place is pretty much one big room. I have privacy issues."

"I've thought about this." Cass got up and walked to the railing overlooking the cabin below. She spread her arms out and turned to look at Erica, who was watching her intently. "We could put a wall up here in place of the railing. This bedroom would be separate from the rest of the house."

"I'm sorry, what?" Erica asked, finally meeting her eyes. "I was a bit distracted by the naked woman parading around."

Cass grinned in response but turned her back to Erica again, looking at the rest of the cabin and sighing. She didn't really want to put a wall up, so she'd have to go with plan B.

"This place is plenty big enough. Danny and I could put up a couple of walls and make a bedroom for Kyle downstairs."

"Come here."

Cass looked over her shoulder and saw Erica had thrown the covers back, and she was patting the space Cass had vacated. She walked back slowly and crawled into the bed with her. Erica wasted no time straddling her.

"If you're sure it's what you want," Erica said, but she didn't sound convinced.

"I'm sure," Cass said. She sucked in a breath when Erica placed her hands on her shoulders and began moving her hips, leaving an intoxicating combination of warmth and wetness on Cass's abdomen. "I wouldn't have suggested it if I wasn't sure."

"Can you have his room ready by the time I bring him home from the hospital?"

"We'll get started on it first thing in the morning."

Cass smiled and ran her hands up Erica's thighs, encouraging her to quicken the pace. When Erica collapsed on top of her a few moments later, completely spent and breathing heavily, Cass held her close, a feeling of pure contentment washing over her. She really was exactly where she belonged.

About the Author

PJ Trebelhorn was born and raised in the greater metropolitan area of Portland, Oregon. Her love of sports (mainly baseball and ice hockey) was fueled in part by her father's interests. She likes to brag about the fact that her uncle managed the Milwaukee Brewers for five years, and the Chicago Cubs for one year.

PJ now resides in western New York with her wife, Cheryl, their four cats, and one very neurotic dog. When not writing or reading, PJ enjoys watching movies, playing on the Playstation, and spending way too much time with stupid games on Facebook. She still roots for the Flyers, Phillies and Eagles, even though she's now in Sabres and Bills territory.

Books Available from Bold Strokes Books

A Touch of Temptation by Julie Blair. Recent law school graduate Kate Dawson's ordained path to the perfect life gets thrown off course when handsome butch top Chris Brent initiates her to sexual pleasure. (978-1-62639-488-9)

Beneath the Waves by Ali Vali. Kai Merlin and Vivien Palmer love the water and the secrets trapped in the depths, but if Kai gives in to her feelings, it might come at a cost to her entire realm. (978-1-62639-609-8)

Girls on Campus edited by Sandy Lowe and Stacia Seaman. College: four years when rules are made to be broken. This collection is required reading for anyone looking to earn an A in sex ed. (978-1-62639-733-0)

Heart of the Pack by Jenny Frame. Human Selena Miller falls for the domineering Caden Wolfgang, but will their love survive Selena learning the Wolfgangs are werewolves? (978-1-62639-566-4)

Miss Match by Fiona Riley. Matchmaker Samantha Monteiro makes the impossible possible for everyone but herself. Is mysterious dancer Lucinda Moss her own perfect match? (978-1-62639-574-9)

Paladins of the Storm Lord by Barbara Ann Wright. Lieutenant Cordelia Ross must choose between duty and honor when a man with godlike powers forces her soldiers to provoke an alien threat. (978-1-62639-604-3)

Taking a Gamble by P.J. Trebelhorn. Storage auction buyer Cassidy Holmes and postal worker Erica Jacobs want different things out of life, but taking a gamble on love might prove lucky for them both. (978-1-62639-542-8)

The Copper Egg by Catherine Friend. Archeologist Claire Adams wants to find the buried treasure in Peru. Her ex, Sochi Castillo, wants to steal it. The last thing either of them wants is to still be in love. (978-1-62639-613-5)

The Iron Phoenix by Rebecca Harwell. Seventeen-year-old Nadya must master her unusual powers to stop a killer, prevent civil war, and rescue the girl she loves, while storms ravage her island city. (978-1-62639-744-6)

A Reunion to Remember by TJ Thomas. Reunited after a decade, Jo Adams and Rhonda Black must navigate a significant age difference, family dynamics, and their own desires and fears to explore an opportunity for love. (978-1-62639-534-3)

Built to Last by Aurora Rey. When Professor Olivia Bennett hires contractor Joss Bauer to restore her dilapidated farmhouse, she learns her heart, as much as her house, is in need of a renovation. (978-1-62639-552-7)

Capsized by Julie Cannon.What happens when a woman turns your life completely upside down? (978-1-62639-479-7)

Girls With Guns by Ali Vali, Carsen Taite, and Michelle Grubb. Three stories by three talented crime writers—Carsen Taite, Ali Vali, and Michelle Grubb—each packing her own special brand of heat. (978-1-62639-585-5)

Heartscapes by MJ Williamz. Will Odette ever recover her memory or is Jesse condemned to remember their love alone? (978-1-62639-532-9)

Murder on the Rocks by Clara Nipper. Detective Jill Rogers lives with two things on her mind: sex and murder. While an ice storm cripples Tulsa, two things stand in Jill's way: her lover and the DA. (978-1-62639-600-5)

Necromantia by Sheri Lewis Wohl. When seeing dead people is more than a movie tagline. (978-1-62639-611-1)

Salvation by I. Beacham. Claire's long-term partner now hates her, for all the wrong reasons, and she sees no future until she meets Regan, who challenges her to face the truth and find love. (978-1-62639-548-0)

Trigger by Jessica Webb. Dr. Kate Morrison races to discover how to defuse human bombs while learning to trust her increasingly strong feelings for the lead investigator, Sergeant Andy Wyles. (978-1-62639-669-2)

24/7 by Yolanda Wallace. When the trip of a lifetime becomes a pitched battle between life and death, will anyone survive? (978-1-62639-619-7)

A Return to Arms by Sheree Greer. When a police shooting makes national headlines, activists Folami and Toya struggle to balance their relationship and political allegiances, a struggle intensified after a fiery young artist enters their lives. (978-1-62639-681-4)

After the Fire by Emily Smith. Paramedic Connor Haus is convinced her time for love has come and gone, but when firefighter Logan Curtis comes into town, she learns it may not be too late after all. (978-1-62639-652-4)

Dian's Ghost by Justine Saracen. The road to genocide is paved with good intentions. (978-1-62639-594-7)

Fortunate Sum by M. Ullrich. Financial advisor Catherine Carter lives a calculated life, but after a collision with spunky Imogene Harris (her latest client) and unsolicited predictions, Catherine finds herself facing an unexpected variable: Love. (978-1-62639-530-5)

Soul to Keep by Rebekah Weatherspoon. What *won't* a vampire do for love… (978-1-62639-616-6)

When I Knew You by KE Payne. Eight letters, three friends, two lovers, one secret. Can the past ever be forgiven? (978-1-62639-562-6)

Wild Shores by Radclyffe. Can two women on opposite sides of an oil spill find a way to save both a wildlife sanctuary and their hearts? (978-1-62639-645-6)

Love on Tap by Karis Walsh. Beer and romance are brewing for Tace Lomond when archaeologist Berit Katsaros comes into her life. (987-1-62639-564-0)

Love on the Red Rocks by Lisa Moreau. An unexpected romance at a lesbian resort forces Malley to face her greatest fears where she must choose between playing it safe or taking a chance at true happiness. (987-1-62639-660-9)

Tracker and the Spy by D. Jackson Leigh. There are lessons for all when Captain Tanisha is assigned untried pyro Kyle and a lovesick dragon horse for a mission to track the leader of a dangerous cult. (987-1-62639-448-3)

Whirlwind Romance by Kris Bryant. Will chasing the girl break Tristan's heart or give her something she's never had before? (987-1-62639-581-7)

Whiskey Sunrise by Missouri Vaun. Culture and religion collide when Lovey Porter, daughter of a local Baptist minister, falls for the handsome thrill-seeking moonshine runner, Royal Duval. (987-1-62639-519-0)

Dyre: By Moon's Light by Rachel E. Bailey. A young werewolf, Des, guards the aging leader of all the Packs: the Dyre. Stable employment—nice work, if you can get it…at least until silver bullets start to fly. (978-1-62639-662-3)

Fragile Wings by Rebecca S. Buck. In Roaring Twenties London, can Evelyn Hopkins find love with Jos Singleton or will the scars of the Great War crush her dreams? (978-1-62639-546-6)

Live and Love Again by Jan Gayle. Jessica Whitney could be Sarah Jarret's second chance at love, but their differences and Sarah's grief continue to come between their budding relationship. (978-1-62639-517-6)

Starstruck by Lesley Davis. Actress Cassidy Hayes and writer Aiden Darrow find out the hard way not all life-threatening drama is confined to the TV screen or the pages of a manuscript. (978-1-62639-523-7)

Stealing Sunshine by Tina Michele. Under the Central Florida sun, two women struggle between fear and love as a dangerous plot of deception and revenge threatens to steal priceless art and lives. (978-1-62639-445-2)

The Fifth Gospel by Michelle Grubb. Hiding a Vatican secret is dangerous—sharing the secret suicidal—can Felicity survive a perilous book tour, and will her PR specialist, Anna, be there when it's all over? (978-1-62639-447-6)

Cold to the Touch by Cari Hunter. A drug addict's murder is the start of a dangerous investigation for Detective Sanne Jensen and Dr. Meg Fielding, as they try to stop a killer with no conscience. (978-1-62639-526-8)

Forsaken by Laydin Michaels. The hunt for a killer teaches one woman that she must overcome her fear in order to love, and another that success is meaningless without happiness. (978-1-62639-481-0)

Infiltration by Jackie D. When a CIA breach is imminent, a Marine instructor must stop the attack while protecting her heart from being disarmed by a recruit. (978-1-62639-521-3)

Midnight at the Orpheus by Alyssa Linn Palmer. Two women desperate to make their way in the world, a man hell-bent on revenge, and a cop risking his career: all in a day's work in Capone's Chicago. (978-1-62639-607-4)

Spirit of the Dance by Mardi Alexander. Major Sorla Reardon's return to her family farm to heal threatens Riley Johnson's safe life when small-town secrets are revealed, and love may not conquer all. (978-1-62639-583-1)